The Secret of Misty Mountain

Robert Lane

authorHOUSE®

AuthorHouse™
1663 Liberty Drive
Bloomington, IN 47403
www.authorhouse.com
Phone: 1-800-839-8640

First published by AuthorHouse   6/21/2011

ISBN: 978-1-4634-1618-8 (sc)
ISBN: 978-1-4634-1617-1 (e)

Chapter I

I'm standing here on the edge of this cliff, located near Misty Mountain, Utah. Misty Mountain is a small town of about 1500 people, located in the mountains about 80 miles from Salt Lake City. I'm looking out over what is normally a very beautiful valley. This night the entire valley is covered by this mysterious mist. How this mist appears has never been seen by anyone before, or how it disappears. It's been a mystery as far back as people can remember. No one has any knowledge of its first appearance, or where it came from. Some people say its clouds; some say its fog, while others say it's a mist. Some even say it's a combination of the three. I remember the first time I saw this mist and the feeling it gave me. It was a very good feeling. I just remember how peaceful it made me feel. Everyone who has seen this mist says exactly the same thing. There have been photographs taken of this mist dating back at least 50 years. In every photograph the pictures of the mist are identical.

I'm standing here alone now, looking at the mist that covers the whole valley. I feel something different tonight, like I was drawn here by some mysterious force. Misty Mountain is one of the top tourist attractions in the United Sates today, so why am I the only one here tonight? Tonight I have a wonderful feeling about myself, a feeling of good and peace. I feel that this could very possibly be my last night on earth as I know it.

I'm going back 15 years and tell of the things that brought me to Misty Mountain. My name is Bob. I grew up in a small mid-western town, as an only child. I loved sports and by participating in these sports, I made a lot of friends. We would always get together and drink some beer after our games. There was one night, I realized something. People love to talk and talk and talk, but I realized very few people listen. I would start to say some-thing, and be interrupted by someone else. So I started talking less and just listened more. I realized that if you say something to someone, it probably won't be heard, but if you put it in writing, like a book or magazine, people would pay more attention to it. So I knew what I wanted to do with my life. I wanted to become a writer, but at this time I didn't know what I wanted to write about. I studied up on the word respect and after a while I discovered many ways in which the word respect could be used. I discovered that most people who use the word respect don't really know the true meaning of the word. To me only good things come from total respect. I found that the word disrespect is more appropriate for most people. By watching television and reading the newspaper and just paying attention to what is going on around me, made me make a list of things in this world I just can't respect. I have no respect for most people in business, any government people or politicians, professional athletes, law officers, law makers, even religion. So I set out to do something good. I took some courses in journalism, to learn how to publish my own work.

I was away at school, when I lost both parents. I will always keep a letter I received form them, telling me how proud they were of me and the future I planned for myself. This letter gave me all the incentive I needed to continue my work. I inherited a lot of money, so I decided to do a lot of traveling, here in the United States, as well as a couple countries over seas. While in the states, I was able to attend a few conventions, for people in journalism. While at one of these conventions, I met Frank. Frank was one of the top bosses for a newspaper in Salt Lake City, Utah. We became friends and stayed in touch with each other.

While traveling through the country, I would always stop near a small town with a lake and campgrounds. This is where I would usually do most of my writing. I was at a lake near a small Midwestern town when I was going over some of my stories, and realized this is not what I wanted to do. Some of the stories were good, but most of them were about the things I disrespected. I was just hoping that something good would come form them. Maybe, later on I could go back and find something good about some of these stories, but not now. Right now all I want to do is find good things to write about.

The next day I called Frank and said I was coming to Salt Lake City and asked if it was Okay to stop by for a visit. He said he would be looking forward to it. I said I would see him in about a week. I made one more stop at a lake, and went over my new stories. I finished with my work in a few days and headed for Salt Lake City. I went to the newspaper where Frank worked. I arrived shortly before he got off work. He invited me over to his house for dinner. We arrived at his house and were met by his wife, Carol, and his son Mark. We had a few minutes before supper was ready, so I filled Frank in on my travels. I just talked about stops at the lakes, where I would camp at and said how relaxing it was to be around nature all the time. Carol called us for dinner, so we sat down and had a terrific meal. I thanked Carol for supper and asked Frank if we could have a talk. I said it would be okay if Mark and Carol joined us. They said they would like that. Frank grabbed a couple beers and we all went outside to the porch.

Frank, raising his can to me said, "Bob, it's good to have a friend stop by. The last we talked, you sounded very interested in what you wanted to do. So fill us in on what you decided."

I replied, "Well where do I start? You know how interested I am in writing, so what I decided to do is publish my own magazine. I only want to write good stories, stories that deserve respect. I had started out writing down things that I find wrong with the world today. Everything was so disrespectful, and I wanted to write things that would make it right. Up until last week, that's what I wanted to do. Now all I want to do write about good things, good things that deserve respect."

"What kind of stories have you written about so far?" asked Carol.

"I have a story on small farmers of our country. These people work hard, long hours during harvest season for only one reason and that is to grow food for the people of the world. I have a story about firemen but only about the firemen who really believe in what they do. There are my stories about animals that made me change my mind about what I really wanted to do. I visited a lot of zoos and saw people who dedicate their lives to the loving and caring of animals. "These people deserve total respect from me," I said.

Frank inquired, "It sounds like you really know what you want to do and if there is anything I can do for you, just let me know. Have you found a place yet? Where you will be doing your work?"

"Not yet, but that is the very thing I want to do." I replied.

Mark joined in the conversation, "Dad, why don't you tell Bob about Misty Mountain? I've been up there a couple times with my friends. We really like to park at the cliff and enjoy the scenery, and other things. Yes, that's right dad – it is also known as lover's lane."

Frank added, "Mark is right! Carol and I have only gone up there once, but it was well worth the trip. There are stories about the cliff and a mysterious mist that has appeared every once in a while. Nobody I know has ever witnessed it but there are a few people from Misty Mountain who have seen it. If you have time, you should drive up there and check it out."

"Misty Mountain? Sounds like a great place to visit, I think I will check it out. Where is it from here?"

"It is about 80 miles north, here take this map." Mark answered.

Carol excused herself and went inside the house. Frank and I continued to talk for another hour as Mark listened. They invited me to stay the night and I accepted. The next morning, Carol had my favorite breakfast prepared bacon and eggs. "Thank you so much for breakfast Carol, which was very good!" I said.

"Thank you Bob, it has been very nice to have one of Franks friends stop by, you are welcome back any time." Carol smiled.

Frank added, "When you find a place to settle down and start your business, please give me a call. I will help you in any way I can."

"I will do that, and thanks to you and family for all being so kind. I am going to make my first stop at Misty Mountain, it sounds like a place I need to see. I will spend about a week before moving on. If I find something interesting to write about, I may stay even longer. I do have a couple other stories I need to finish as well. They are from my travels overseas, those will get published first. If I do come up with some good human interest stories, I will call you. Who knows, you may be able to use them for your newspaper." I told Frank.

"Thank you Bob, that would be great. We can work together in our line of business." Frank replied.

We said our goodbyes and I drove off on my way toward Misty Mountain. The road was two-lane without much traffic so the trip took a little over an hour. When I reached Misty Mountain, the first thing I did was find a motel. I then took a walk through the streets in town to familiarize myself with the town. I really liked what I saw; the scenery was beautiful and made me feel welcome. The way the town was arranged left little room for expansion. It had little shops like you would expect in am older, small town. I found a photo shop and went inside to drop off some film. The couple who owned the store was very nice. I told them I would be around for about a week so there was no rush. I left there and walked to a diner to get something to eat. It was called Mike and Tina's diner. There were a couple tourists eating and visiting with Tina. She was showing them pictures of the cliff and telling them of the mist that covers the valley. So, when I finished eating, I asked her to show me the photos and while showing them to me, her husband, Mike, came and joined us. They spoke about what a tourist attraction this mysterious mist had become. Mike said that the cliff was only a mile up the road and that I could drive or walk. He pointed me in the right direction and I left the diner heading toward the edge of town. On my way out of town I noticed the local bar and thought to myself, "I will see you tonight!"

I reached the cliff and scenery was beautiful. Off in the distance I could see some snow capped mountains. There was a small lake that looked so peaceful, that I knew I was going to spending some time there. I took out my camera and began taking shots of the valley below. I walked to the edge and sat down. A feeling of peace and goodness overwhelmed me as I enjoyed this amazing view for hours. As the sun started to set, I decided it was time to head back to town. I arrived at the hotel, unpacked a few things, showered and headed out to the bar.

I walked in, sat down and ordered a beer. I didn't say anything to anyone, I just wanted to sit and listen. The bar was not crowded; there were maybe 20 people there. As it got later, people started clearing out and before I knew it I was the last one there. The bar tender asked me if I would like one more beer before shut down for the night.

"Only if I can buy you one." I answered, "Your name is Tom, right?"

"Yes, I'm Tom, and that would be great to sit and have a beer with you, thanks! And you are?" Tom was holding out his hand to shake mine.

"Bob, I just arrived in town today and plan on being around for about a week. The scenery around here is great!"

"Yes I agree, my wife, Barb, and I love it here, so what brings you to Misty Mountain?"

"I am hoping to start a business. I want to publish my own magazine and am shopping for a good location. A friend of mine suggested coming up here after I told him about my plans. He thought it would be a great place to write about. So I am going spend some time talking to people about the cliff and the mist that I have heard so much about." I answered.

"That sounds very interesting; I'd like to read that, if you don't mind. There have only been good things said about the cliff and the mist. It would make a great story. If you have any questions in mind, just stop back in here tonight and there will be a few people in here that might be able to help you out." Tom replied.

We were just finishing our beers when a woman came in.

"Bob, I would like you to meet my wife, Barb. Honey, this is Bob."

"Hi Bob, it is nice to meet you." Barb said with a friendly smile on her face.

"It is great to meet you too Barb. I was just getting ready to leave, but I will be back again tomorrow. Maybe we can sit down and talk. I have a ton of questions. I'll see you tomorrow, if that is OK with you."

I left the bar and went back to the motel. I opened another beer, sat down and relaxed. It was a good day. I made a few notes, finished my beer and went to bed. I woke up around 9:00, showered and left for the diner. After breakfast I decided to drive up to the cliff today. When I got to the cliff, I found a nice place to park. I took out my lawn chair, a pad and pen. I walked over to the edge, sat my chair down and began taking notes. I took a lot of pictures and was there most of the morning by myself. About noon I was joined by a couple tourists, very nice people. We talked for a couple hours and they left for their next destination. I stayed until about an hour before sunset, while writing down my last few notes when some local teens began to arrive. I packed everything up and drove back into town. I went back to the motel and went over some of my notes while drinking a beer. I then headed to the bar.

The bar was crowded tonight but I found a place to sit at the bar.

"Hi Bob, how was your day?" I heard Tom's voice.

I replied, "I had a fantastic day. If you have time later on, I would love to talk it over with you, when you are not busy. I see you are helping Barb, this place is busy tonight."

"This is one of our busiest nights, but it is also a night that people leave early so Barb and I usually order a pizza while cleaning up and take it home with us. You are welcome to join us this evening if you would like."

"I would love it. Pizza is my favorite food. Please, let me buy both the pizza and some beer tonight, it would be my pleasure."

Tom nodded, "You're on. You are going to love this pizza. There is a family in town that makes pizzas at their house. Everything is freshly made from scratch and loaded with whatever ingredients you order. It takes about 45 minutes to an hour but well worth the wait. Jack and Sarah are the couple who make the pizzas. We will stop by and pick it up on our way home. They are pretty good about knowing who their regulars are and when they will be ordering so they don't have much waste. If they anything left over at night – they will use up the ingredients making pizzas and freezing them, for which they will charge less but I don't know why, they taste just as good as the fresh ones if you ask me. Everyone in town has the deepest respect for them and never complains about having to wait. You will see tonight how good their pizza is."

"I can't wait!" I replied.

I sat around the rest of the night, talking to some of the local people Tom introduced me to. Tom was right. The bar did empty out early. Barb ordered the pizza and I helped them clean up. It was hard for me to believe that people could be so nice to a person they had just met. In just a couple days, I found two people who I could truly respect. Maybe there is a lot more good in this world than bad. These are the kind of people I am looking for to write stories about. They finished cleaning up and we went to get the pizzas and head to their house. Tom and I went out back since it was such a beautiful evening and Barb soon followed with pizza and beer.

"Well Bob, did you learn anything today about our cliff and the mist?" Tom asked.

"I did learn a lot today." Smiling at them and telling them about the respect I had for them. "While on the cliff today, I did a lot of thinking. I thought about what I was doing and where I was headed." I answered that last question myself. "I couldn't think of a more perfect place than Misty Mountain to publish my magazine. I think living here would be perfect for me. I am going to start looking tomorrow for a place to live."

"I know of a couple houses up for sale right now. One is available right away, the couple moved out a couple months ago and the other will be available at the end of the year. I can show you them tomorrow if you are free." Barb said.

"Barb is one of the most helpful people you will ever meet." Tom said. "If you need anything at all, help from anyone, just let her know and she will point you in the direction."

"Well, thank you both very much, and you were right, this pizza is awesome! If you two aren't busy tomorrow morning, say around 10, I would like to buy you breakfast at the diner. Somehow I feel this is first day of the rest of my life." I said.

"Thanks Bob, 10 it is, we will be there." Tom answered.

It was getting late. Tom asked me if I needed a ride back to the motel. I told him it was such a beautiful night and I would enjoy a nice walk. We said good night and I walked back to the motel.

The next morning I met Tom and Barb at the diner. There, they introduced me to Mike and Tina who has ran the diner for 15 years, so they know everyone in town. We finished breakfast and Tom said he was headed for the bar. Barb and I went to check out the house that would be available right away. It was absolutely perfect for me, not too big, not too small. It also had a big back yard that I really loved because I wanted to get a dog soon. I told Barb it was perfect and asked who I talk to buy it. She knew the person I needed to talk with, his name was Bill. She said we could walk over to this office, so we did. On our way there, I asked her if she knew of any vacant buildings available As luck would have it, we would be passing one on our way to Bill's office. She pointed it out as we approached the next block and it too looked absolutely perfect. I asked if Bill could help me with both the house and the building and she said that he could. When we got to Bill's, Barb introduced us and then had to leave to run her errands. Bill and I had a long talk and he was able to help me with the house and leasing the building. He asked me to stop back in a couple days later and he would have all the paperwork ready for me to go over. I left his office and went to bar to see Tom. He was just getting ready to open.

"Hi Tom." I said, "I want to thank you and Barb for all your help. I am going to buy the house and lease a building Barb showed me this morning, I think both will be just perfect for what I have planned."

"That is great news Bob." Tom replied and added, "Looks like we will be seeing a lot of you around here. Have a beer on me."

"Thanks Tom, and yes, I am now one of your regulars. By the way, I don't drink much but I do drink often. What we drank last night was about my limit, I don't drink to get drunk, just to relax."

"We were both laughing when Barb walked in.

"Hi honey, hi Bob, how did things go with Bill?" she asked

Grinning from ear to ear, I replied, "Just great! I have decided to buy the house and lease the building. Bill said he will have it all worked out for me in just a couple days. There is something I would like to share with both of you that is a tradition of mine, I would like the both of you to join me in a toast. When something good happens, I like to toast a beer with my friends. So to my new friends, who have been so helpful and friendly to me, a total stranger, this toast is for you." Tom gave Barb a beer and we all three held our glasses together and toasted to our new friendship.

"My very first story will be about Misty Mountain, the town, the people and the cliff with the mysterious mist. It is going be a great story, I have a feeling."

I didn't stay long. I went back to the motel, sat down and started jotting down thoughts and ideas about my first story. I figured I would be spending a lot of time at the cliff for inspiration. It is such a perfect place to relax a place of peace and perfect to do my work.

The next two weeks flew by, I was so busy. Bill and I finalized all the paperwork for both properties. I ordered furniture for the house, and office supplies and furniture for the building. I met a guy named Steve who was the construction manager of a small company in Misty Mountain. He was going to be helping me with some remodeling in the building once he finished up another job he was working on. I told him not to hurry; I would never pressure him with a deadline.

I called my friend Frank and informed him of my progress here in Misty Mountain and invited him to come visit soon. He told me he would love to and could probably get away in about three weeks.

Chapter 11

Three weeks went by and sure enough, there was a knock at my door and when I answered, there he was, along with Mark.

"Hi Bob." Frank said, "Hope you don't mind but Mark wanted to tag along."

I was happy to see them both. I shook their hands and said, 'No problem, you are both welcome any time, come this way, I will show you my office. We can sit down in there and have a talk. I have some questions for you."

"Sure thing." Frank answered, "This really is a beautiful town, and I can see why you want to stay here."

We walked into my office and sat down. I offered them drinks and started talking. For knew exactly who I wanted but wasn't sure if he would be interested. I called Frank and told him I was coming down to talk to him and Mark. By staying in touch with Frank I learned a little about Mark. During his high school years, he was working part time for the newspaper, not because his dad worked there but it was something he was very interested in doing. When he was off duty, he'd be down in the press room just hanging out. He became great friends with the boss. The boss really liked Mark because Mark took such and interest in what they did. Mark was fascinated with the press room and he was always asking questions about how things worked. After Mark graduated form high school he went to work full time for the newspaper. It was right after he started full time that a job became open in the press room. Other people applied but Mark got the job. Others thought it was just because his dad worked there but based on enthusiasm alone, the boss knew he made the right decision. He was treated badly by his co-workers at first who would not talk to him much and showed a lot of disrespect toward him. Mark did not let that bother him though; he showed up every day and did his job. Frank was very proud of the way he carried himself.

I arrived in Salt Lake City and went straight to Frank's house. Frank was the only one there when I arrived. It gave me a chance to talk with him alone before Mark and Carol come home a bit later. I then got a chance to speak with Mark alone and then we all four sat down to talk.

With a smile on my face, I looked at Mark. "Mark, I have a proposition for you. I am looking for someone to come work for me. Your knowledge of presses makes me think of you first. I don't need an answer right away but would like to tell you a little about how I run things and then let you decide. First of all I need someone that will have complete control of the pressing operations. It would be a low stress job for you, working for me; I like to take my time to do things right so deadlines are non-existent. We would simply work together and have fun doing it. I would like to offer whatever you make now, and double it, I know you are worth it! You wouldn't be that far from home so you could come home to visit your parents any time you like. I know I am throwing this at you kind of quickly but please take some time and think about it."

Mark had a surprised look on his face as he looked over at his parents and Frank spoke up, "We can discuss this but I have already talked with Bob and I think this is a great opportunity. The decision is yours; you know your mother and I will support you in whatever you decide."

"I don't know what to say, this gives me a lot to think about. I will let you know Bob." Said Mark.

"If you decide to accept my offer, I will help you find a place to live. I've also got a dog who loves people so you will never be alone. I have given you a lot to think about so I will leave you alone and hope to hear from you soon." I said.

I drove back home, thinking all the way how great it would be if Mark accepted. When I got back to Misty Mountain, I stopped at the bar for a couple beers then went on home.

Two weeks went by and finally both Frank and Mark walked into my office.

"Hi Bob" Mark said, "I've decided to take you up on your offer, I think it would be an honor to come work with you, when can I start?"

"That is great news, you can start right away. You can stay at my place tonight and I can show you around tomorrow. I am so happy you have accepted, thanks for making my day! Let's make a toast, you like beer don't you Mark?"

"I don't drink much but a nice cold beer once in a while is great. Dad told me how you like to toast with beer, so I would be honored to join you." Mark replied.

"Good." I said, "Here is to us Mark, and many more toasts to come."

The next morning, the three of us went to breakfast. Then I took the two of them back to my office. Frank would be leaving soon, so I showed them around the work area and warehouse. Frank liked what I had done to the place so far and Mark too, was very impressed. Frank had to leave to get back home so Mark and I sat down to talk.

"OK Mark, rule number one, no suits or ties!" I laughed, "There are no more rules at this time. Feel free to make up some notes on everything you see. I really want to know your opinion, especially back in the warehouse. You can set things up the way they work for you, you alone, are in charge. If you have any questions, let me know. I will grab us a pizza for lunch and we can sit and talk. If anyone comes in, feel free to introduce yourself, see you later."

I came back later with the pizza. Mark got us a couple sodas from the cooler and we sat down to go over the notes Mark had been making. He was very familiar with the press I had. He made some notes on simplifying the set up. I knew he was going to be very efficient and an asset to me.

A year had passed. We had published two more magazines. For a while Mark was spending almost every weekend driving to Salt Lake to visit friends and family. The more time he spent reading the stories though, the more he found himself staying home and helping me. He even wrote a story himself, a very good one.

It was early summer the next year and Mark and I had just finished another publication. We were doing inventory after shipping our latest magazine out to our subscribers when the door opened and in walked a young girl and older man.

"Hi, my name is Lorrie and this is my grandfather." Said the young girl.

"Hello, my name is Bob and this is Mark. Please have a seat, would you like something to drink?"

Lorrie motioned to her grandfather, "Yes we would like that very much. We have just arrived from New Mexico, it was a long trip."

"What brings you to Misty Mountain?" I asked.

"Well, I just graduated from high school and my grandfather here has always told me after graduation there was something he wanted me to do. So he asked me to drive him here, to Misty Mountain, Utah. I was raised by grandpa as my parents both died at a young age. I love and respect him very much so was glad to honor his request."

Lorrie's grandfather leaned close to her and spoke in a very low voice to her. Lorrie looked up and said, "Grandfather would like you to take him to the place of the mist."

"I would love to; don't you want to rest a while first? I can get some food together and we can have a nice picnic up there. The sun will be setting in about 3 hours and would be the perfect time for us to be there."

Lorrie's grandfather nodded in agreement and Lorrie said, "He does not talk much because he doesn't speak English very well, but he does understand us." Just then Star walked in and went right up to the old man and put her paw in his lap, she really took a liking to him.

Mark left to pick up the food and came back just in time for us to leave. We all got in my car and drove up to the cliff. As we arrived, we spotted an available picnic table so we all sat down there to eat. Star ran around and played and after we finished a nice meal, the four of us walked over to the cliff to watch the sunset.

"This is my favorite spot, I like to sit here and enjoy the scenery. I also come up here to do a lot of my writing. Let me get out some lawn chairs for you all, we will be here for a while."

Grandfather motioned for Lorrie to come to his side. He spoke again in a low voice. Lorrie looked at Mark and I, "Grandfather would like to be left alone here for a while, is that OK?"

Mark and I agreed, as we were walking away – Star decided to stay by the old man's side. We packed everything up and drove back into town. Mark Lorrie and I sat down back at the office and made ourselves comfortable.

"Lorrie, have you read our magazines?" asked Mark. "The reason I am asking is because I just wrote a story on Native Americans and it was in our latest edition. Let me get you a copy."

"Lorrie, do you know why your grandfather asked you to drive him up here?" I asked.

"No I don't and I don't believe I have ever heard of your magazine. My grandfather doesn't read much but is very interested in the cliff. Can you tell me why?" Lorrie asked.

"The cliff is very special, there is a mist that appears once in a while but neither of us has witnessed that yet. We do have some photos of it though." I handed her some pictures, "Do you think your grandfather has seen pictures of this mist?"

Mark brought out a stack of magazines, every one we have published and gave them to Lorrie. "Here you go, something for you to read when you get a chance. Here is the one about the cliff and the mist. Maybe your grandfather knows something about it. If he does, we would sure like to know."

"It is probably time to go back and pick him up; it is getting kind of late." I said.

"No not yet, he is fine and wanted some time alone, so let's give him another hour or so." Lorrie replied

"OK, tell us something about yourself. What are your interests? Now that you have graduated, what are you plans?" I asked her.

"I haven't given it much thought, I made straight A's all through school and have been offered a couple scholarships to continue my education, yet I am still undecided. I want to stay close to home and take care of grandfather."

We talked some more and I found her very intelligent and interesting. At one point she looked at her watch and said, "It is time to go get grandfather now. Thank you both for being so nice, and thanks for the magazines. I will read them, I promise."

We drove up to the cliff and found Grandfather and Star waiting right where we left them. They got in and we drove back to town. I invited Lorrie and her Grandfather to spend the night at my house and they accepted. The next morning I made a big breakfast and then Grandfather told Lorrie that he wanted to speak to me alone. Lorrie agreed and began gather up their things and loading them in their car.

"I hope you had a nice visit Grandfather. Can you tell me what brought you to Misty Mountain? You must have a good reason and I would love to hear it."

He looked at me with a huge smile on his face. There was something in his eyes that told me what I wanted to know. He stood up, shook my hand and said goodbye.

I had to ask, "You saw the list last night, didn't you?"

He nodded his head up and down, smiled again and waved goodbye as he got into the car with Lorrie. They drove away as I watched.

About six months had passed. Mark and I were sitting in the office one day when Lorrie walked through the door. She didn't look happy like the first time we met.

"Hi Mark, hi Bob." She said.

"Well, Lorrie, it is great to see you. Did you bring your grandfather with you?"

"No." she replied, with tears in her eyes she continued, "He passed away just two weeks ago. I was by his side until he was gone." She started to sob, "The last thing he told me was that I should return the Misty Mountain and work with you guys. When I asked him why, he just smiled, squeezed my hand and then he was gone."

"Mark and I walked over to her and gave her a hug. "I'm so sorry, please, if there is anything at all we can do, you will let us know, anything." I said.

"Grandfather was a very wise man and I loved and respected him. I know there is a reason he told me to come here and I'm sure I will find out some day but for right now, I am confused and nervous." Lorrie said.

"Lorrie, I am probably just as confused as you are, but I think I understand. Your grandfather told me he had seen the mist when he was here. I really think he knew something about it. He felt the same way about it, that everyone who sees it feels it. It is supposedly a great feeling. I think he believed and with your help, we can also find the secret to Misty Mountain. You have a job here if you want it. We would be very proud to have you work with us."

Lorrie stayed with me for a couple days. I showed her around the town the same way I was shown, and in turn showed Mark around. We found her a nice little place and she went back home to get the rest of her belongings. Mark went with her to help out. It was like an addition to our family. She was at home with us and we helped her get settled.

Lorrie loved her new home and her neighbors and soon everyone in town got to know how wonderful she was. We spent the first two weeks just going over everything in the office. Mark showed her the press and the instructions on how to operate it. Lorrie stood in front of the press and read each of the steps Mark had written down. She had very high praise for Mark. She had no experience with this type of work but Marks attention to detail made it very easy for her to learn. Visuals in the workplace are beneficial in teaching others and Lorrie explained to Mark that if more people would use this type of training, it would be a much simpler world.

I told Lorrie that everything we do here is done with a lot of patience. We will never be in a hurry. We have to ensure our work is true and correct, quality is more important than quantity. There are no deadlines on any story we publish. I explained to her that at no time will we ever run our business like others. We will take the time to teach and be very patient about it. It will not be like corporate America where time is money and the word patience does not exist. I like to make people feel appreciated and stress free.

Six months had passed. Lorrie had caught on quickly and she and Mark worked very well together. Sometimes they would cover for each other, Mark would be working on a story and Lorrie would take care of the press and warehouse. They liked the versatility and the three of us were great together.

One Friday morning I could hear Mark and Lorrie having a little disagreement on something in the warehouse. I quickly called them into the office. "It's Friday morning," I said. "Why don't we call it a week? But first of all, I want us to sit down and talk for a while. I want to help you both with something called respect. I stopped you in the middle of a slight disagreement. Do you know that a big argument will almost always begin with a little disagreement? Stop me if I'm wrong here, but I did over hear you two arguing, I don't know what it was about but that really doesn't matter. By using a little respect for each other we can resolve what ever it is. I know, I wrote an article on this very subject when I first began witting. Mark, you go first and Lorrie, please don't say anything until Mark is finished and just listen carefully. When Mark is finished then you will have your chance as well. I will not interrupt unless you both start talking at the same time again. I've learned that when two people are talking at the same time, neither is really listening and things can get said that you really don't mean and then the argument escalates. Okay Mark, go ahead and begin."

Mark explained himself and said all he wanted to say as Lorrie listened. I watched them both very closely. When he finished, Lorrie said her piece as Mark listened. When she finished I asked them both to sit quietly and just think about what they heard form each other. I understand now that this was work related so explained to both of them that they can always come to me for a third opinion, but if it was a personal conflict, they would have to settle it themselves. I also went on to tell them that if the problem is settled by just the two of them that they can learn from this experience. By listening to each other and showing mutual respect, you can settle an argument before it happens. I said we're going to close up for about three hours. I wanted to take Star up to the cliff and get a little exercise and we could meet back at the office later. We all left together. I was at the cliff playing with Star and two hours later, here came Mark and Lorrie.

Lorrie got out of the car and said, "It didn't take me long to realize that I was wrong in the way I approached Mark. You were right Bob, just by listening and not interrupting can make you see things a lot differently. We came up here to let you know we have come to an agreement without needing a third opinion.

"I had a feeling you wouldn't need my input, just a little guidance. We have all been working together for a while now and I am very impressed with you both. Today you have learned something very important about respect. It is easy to get carried away with your own thoughts and forget to listen. I just didn't want what was just a little disagreement to turn into a huge argument. I just care a lot about the both of you and I want us to stay together for a long time." I explained.

"Thank you so much Bob." Lorrie replied. "I have learned from you today and so has Mark. I love you both and enjoy working with you as well. We make a great team, the three of us and someday we will all make a difference in this world. My grandfather was a very wise man and I knew he wanted me to come here for a reason. I don't know what that is yet but I plan to stay as long as that takes." Lorrie looked at Mark and I together and continued, "I think this is a perfect time for a toast."

For the next few months things were even better than before. We had fun at work and were just like a family. One day the office door opened and in walked a young, very pretty lady.

"Hi, I was hoping to get a picture of the three of you. Could you move close together? There, that's perfect." She snapped a picture and as she turned to walk out the door, said, "Thank you very much."

None of us had a chance to say a word. We all just looked at each other. A few minutes later, the door opened again and she re-entered, this time with Tom.

Tom, with his arm around the young lady said, "I tried to get here in time to warn you but I was little too late. I hope my little sister didn't offend you. She's always had a funny way of doing things. Bob, Lorrie, Mark, I'd like you to meet my little sister, Brittany."

"Brittany, what a pretty name, have a seat, can I get you something to drink?" I asked. Lorrie handed her a Pepsi and said, "Please tell us about yourself."

"Well, now you know I am Tom's little sister. I grew up here and when I graduated from high school I moved out east to go to college. I used to work at the photo store part time before I moved and I really liked it so I decided to pursue an education in a photography field. So I now am done with college and the couple that runs the photo store here in town called me to let me know they are selling it. What great timing! They wanted to give me first dibs on buying it, so I jumped at it. It is great to be back home. I am also very impressed with your work, especially the story on Misty Mountain and the cliff. I did grow up here, but have never been lucky enough to see the mist. I have tons of pictures though and thought maybe you would like to use more photos and colors in your magazine."

"We would love to take a look at them. I like her, can we keep her?" Lorrie asked.

We all laughed and then I said, "I think that would be great for us to work together, I like the idea of more pictures."

As the months went by, Brittany became close to us all and she did great work on photos. It was the Friday before Christmas and this year I decided not to buy gifts as I had done in the past, instead I wanted to make a special announcement. I informed both Mark and Lorrie that they were, as of the first of the year, full partners in the business. I handed them both envelopes with the legal papers. "We are all equal now. I have grown to love a respect you both and don't want to lose either of you. So now it is our company!" I also added, "Brittany, you have done great work with us and I would like to put you on the pay roll full time if you are interested."

Brittany agreed and we went on from there. Over the next couple years we all bonded even more. Lorrie and Brittany were best friends. Tom and Barb were expecting their first child and Barb worked at the photo store for Brittany and freed her up to work for us more often. She even set up a nursery in an empty area in the back of the photo shop so Barb can bring the baby to work.

I began spending more time up on the cliff. One night in the early fall, Star and I were up there for an early snowfall, and it was beautiful. Star loved to play in the snow, there was about 3 inches on the ground and it was snowing lightly. We were all alone up there and spent about an hour. It started to get pretty cold so I called for Star to get in the car. As we started up the car, Star just started barking out of the blue. I didn't know what was wrong with him but opened his door so he could get out. He ran to the edge of the cliff and just sat down. I called for him to come back but he didn't budge so I walked to the edge to get him and my mouth dropped and my eyes widened as I looked out over the valley, it was the mist. Star seemed so peaceful just sitting there looking at it too. It was very mysterious. I ran to the car to grab the camera and began taking pictures like crazy, from all angles, until I was all out of film. I went back to the car to see if I had any more in my camera bag and as I was sitting there, Star came up and jumped in the car, licked my face and lay down in his seat. I walked back over to the edge of the cliff to look out and I saw that the mist was completely gone. It went away as fast as it appeared. I found the extra film and took a few more pictures. Then we left for home.

The next day at the office I showed the photos to Mark, Lorrie and Brittany. I told them about my exciting night. "I've never asked this of any of you, but I am going to ask a favor. What I want you to do is stop whatever it is you are working on right now and all of us work together on another story about the mist. Brittany, I will need you to go through all the pictures I took and pick out the best of the best and Lorrie I want you to do the story."

"I don't know Bob, I would love nothing more than another story about the mist but now that you have seen it, don't you think you should write about it? I will be glad to help though." Said Lorrie.

I smiled at her and added, "Not this time Lorrie, I did one already, before I saw the mist. I have faith that you can write this one on what you feel. Go through the pictures for inspiration, take your time and use your instincts and creativity. If you need to dig deep for something good, then use what ever you learned form your grandfather. I know you can do this and make it really special. There is just something about this mist, something very special and even though I finally got to see it, I still don't have a clue. So let's get to work."

Lorrie replied, "Bob, I appreciate your confidence in me and I will not let you down. I'm not sure if this is the right time to bring this up but Mark and I found some of your old stories in the back room and were going through them. We want to use them, do something with them. What do you think?"

"Those stories are about things I see wrong in this world today. I kept them hoping someday I could use them. They are about respect. When I moved here I realized that I would no longer need them. What is it about them that you like?"

"Oh Bob, there are some great stories in there!" Mark said. "Lorrie and I talked about them and we came up with the idea to do a special, separate edition. We would not let it affect the work we are doing now and we want to handle all the expenses ourselves."

I thought for a minute and added, "You both realize that those articles were written to show disrespect to almost every kind of organization on this planet. They are the exact opposite of what we do now and we are becoming very popular for our positive writings, according to the fan mail. If we were to print those articles, don't you think the response will also be negative?"

Brittany, who was quiet up until now chimed in, "I read them too Bob and I have to say I agree with Lorrie and Mark. If we get hate mail in return doesn't that mean we are making people aware of the disrespectable articles that they read? If something good were to come of it, people will see it another way. The subject of disrespect will help our peace through respect magazine and they will both help sell each other."

"That is a good point Brittany but one of the reasons I didn't follow through with those articles was because one of every hundred people who would read them may actually do something about it. People just don't care but if you think you can change that, then more power to you. Let's not let it interfere with our magazine right now, lets get ready to begin the next issue. Lorrie, take your time on this one and any time we all need to sit and talk about it let us know. Are you all ready to get started?"

Brittany stood up and yelled excitedly, "Yes! I can't wait to get started on this, and Bob, I think this is a perfect time for a toast!"

The next week went by quickly. Mark and I finished with the back room and the press was set up and ready to go. Brittany was helping Lorrie with the story and they finished it in ten days. It was a Friday morning when Lorrie asked Mark and me to take a look at it. So Mark read it and liked it very much. So I took it and sat down and began to read. It was excellent and the picture layout was amazing. I was very pleased. I ordered some pizza and we all had another toast.

We had finished running the last page when Brittany and Lorrie came into the press room. Brittany wanted to show me the cover she made for the edition. It was so beautiful. It included an arrangement of dogs, and the best one was Star sitting at the cliff looking over the valley at the mist. I absolutely loved it! This was the first time we had all worked together on the assembly and shipping. We finally got it all done and mailed out to our subscribers.

A couple weeks went by and I was going to the bar one evening. Lorrie, Mark and Brittany were already there and the bar was pretty crowded this night. We had some tourists in town and everyone was laughing and having a real good time. I got my beer and joined my three partners. I sat down and asked them what was going on tonight.

"We were just talking about some of the disrespect articles and others were listening to our conversation and pretty soon everybody began telling us their own version of things that they have witnessed in regards to disrespect. You should hear what some had to say, we are just getting started Bob, so just listen. Everybody – this is Bob and that was his article on sports we were talking about." Mark explained.

One of the tourists remarked, "Nice to meet you Bob. Everything you wrote is so true. What you said about professional football players was right on target. You turn on the TV and what do you see? Grown men who make a handsome paycheck doing their stupid dances and other antics on the field. The fans love it, the media loves it, I just don't understand. We all got a laugh on your quote though, if only these players spent as much time studying the game plan as they do figuring out what stupid dance they plan to do, they may have a better chance of winning the game."

"You are so very right." I said. "It's the stupid things they do that do not gain any type of respect from me. It's not just the players either, the media has to replay it over and over and the sportscasters talk about it. I need to add something to that article. We all know that it's all about the money. It is a business and should be treated as one. You hire someone to do a job and if they don't show up on their first day or the next day, what are the chances you will still let this person work for you? None, zero – they would be fired. So, in sports, if anyone does not want to come to the first day of practice and does not want to even practice at all with the team, then they should be fired. They are all so over paid it is a joke! I mean, get real! Most rookies want more for their first season than a middle class person makes their whole life! I think they should be paid for what they do, their performance. It makes sense to me that they should be paid after the job is done just like everyone else."

"You are right Bob!" Another person added, "If we could just rid this disease, we could actually have real sports again. The fans could have a lot to do in getting reality back into it too, but they won't. They might complain about it around the water coolers at work but that's it. I think just one game, an opening game of the season, no one should attend, buy tickets, except one person, and they could sit in the stands with a huge sign saying 'OWNERS AND PLAYERS TAKE A GOOD LONG LOOK AT YOUR FUTURE!' Just the first home game of the season that would make an impact!"

Another person stood up to add their two cents in, "I have always been a baseball fan, there are things that happen every day that pisses me off!

I cannot believe the pitchers that intentionally throw the ball at a batter. That could really hurt someone badly and all they get out of it is a warning. When the teams actually have an all out brawl, some of them end up with fines, but with the money they make, it is only a slap on the hand. Maybe a batter should take a big a swing and let the bat go into the direction of the pitcher, send him a message, 'If you throw at me, then I am going to throw at you!'"

Several people laughed at that statement, then a woman chimed in, "I'm having a lot of fun here listening to the bar talk, the sports world sure doesn't earn the respect that most fans do give, nor do they even care. Aside form sports, what about the laws, the judicial system? I am under the influence right now, after two beers, so cannot drive home. I think there should be a difference between under the influence and all out drunk. The penalties are the same though; I would be over the legal limit and not be drunk in my opinion. I grew up learning safe driving habits and have a clean record and feel I will be just fine driving home tonight, but the law sees it a different way. If there is an accident, alcohol related or not, that is the first thing they ask. I think most accidents are just bad driving habits. I actually would feel safer driving myself home than to be with someone, maybe a member of MADD, driving down the road, 10 to 20 miles over the speed limit talking on their cell phone. Do fellow police officers treat their co-workers in the same manner as they would you and I? Some? Maybe, but most I think not. I just don't trust them for the most part. Total respect is something that is earned."

Coming from the bar, a man adds his piece, "I have no respect for our government or politicians who run this country. I really love this country but the people who run it are dishonest and only tell us what they want us to hear. What they do not say are the things that make me have no respect for them. It seems like they cover up a lot of stuff, it's all about money or power to them."

A lady tourist stood up and said, "My husband and I have had a small business in Chicago for about 15 years and we came here to see Misty Mountain, and the valley where the mist appears. We have made good living from our business but there are things that have held us back that leads us to have no respect for larger businesses and corporations. They are all about putting us out of business for their own selfishness. It's all about greed with them. That may be pretty smart on their side; we all want to make money. It is the way they go about it that makes me hate them. Bob, you don't know us but we are big fans of your magazine and the way you run it. My husband is a lot like you, he doesn't look scruffy by any means, and he has nice jeans. He is against wearing a tie, like you. I mean, what does a tie do for you anyway? I just don't get it, but that is what people need to get further in the business world, a tie and a degree. I think experience and common sense should mean more than a tie and a degree, but that just isn't the way it is but that is why they do not have my respect!"

Tom rang the bell and shouted, "Last Call! I have heard a lot this evening; it's been great hearing all the opinions. It's been a fun night, I hope you can all come back tomorrow night, I can't wait to hear more."

Lorrie, Mark, Brittany and I left together.

"I think you got a lot of material to work with on your magazine." I said.

"All the things I heard tonight made me think of just how many ways a person can view just what disrespect means." Brittany said. "I can't even say that I disagree with any of the points brought up tonight."

Lorrie said, "Sometimes when you listen to people talk about things you think they are full of bull. By showing respect and actually hearing what people have to say, you can find some truth in what they are saying. I think I now know how we can make our work more informative to our readers. I don't think we can be as honest with our magazine as we can our 'Peace Thru Respect' magazine. We will have to stick to opinions of other people."

"You three have matured so much in the few years I have known you." I said. "I have the deepest respect for you and I'm sure you will always do the right thing. I was impressed with the job all of you did on our latest edition. The story was beautiful. Brittany, what you did with the pictures was absolutely perfect. We have received some very good responses from our readers. Sales are already climbing."

We all said our good nights and went home.

About 3 weeks went by and one morning Star and I stopped at the diner for breakfast. Lorrie was there so we had breakfast together. Mike gave Star his usual snack and we then walked to the office. Mark and Brittany were already there.

"Hey you guys, check this out!" Mark said while going through messages on the computer, "Bob there is a message here from Mr. Chang."

"Who is Mr. Chang?" Brittany asked.

"Mr. Chang is a friend of mine, he lives in China." I answered, he does the same kind of work we do, only in his country. He has visited the U.S. a few times and speaks very good English, as well as a couple other languages. A few years ago he read one of our copies and called me. I invited him to Misty Mountain but he hasn't made it yet. We gave each other numbers and addresses and kept in touch. We exchange stories, good stories and have been helping each other get our magazines out world wide. Now there are 12 people in our group and all speak English, the list of them and where they live is in my office. I don't believe any of us have actually met face to face but it is a great feeling that there are 12 countries covered in our endeavor to only write about good things in this world. So, what does Mr. Chang have to say Mark?"

"He didn't get right down to it Bob, but he does sound excited about something."

"Maybe it is important, what time is it? Okay, if you guys are interested in hearing what he has to say, come back tonight when I call him. Lets' take the afternoon off; I think I will take Star up to the cliff. If anyone wants to join us, you are welcome. I can grab a pizza on the way."

We all went to the cliff together that day. It was very nice weather and allowed us all to relax. Time flew by though. Before we knew it, it was time to go back to the office and call Mr. Chang. I used the speaker phone so everyone could hear.

"Hello Mr. Chang. It's Bob here, returning your call."

"Hi Bob, it's been a while, how are you doing?"

"We are doing just fine; did you get a copy of our latest magazine?" I replied.

"Yes I did, that is why I called. In my last issue I used the story you did on the cliff by Misty Mountain. I really liked the pictures of your dog."

"That article was written by Lorrie, and the picture arrangement was done by Brittany." I explained. "Isn't it great to be able share such wonderful stories? I think people like to read about good things and am so happy we share that point of view." I added.

"I feel the same way Bob." Mr. Chang said. "The reason I called you is, well it might not be anything but I received a call from a man in the west part of China. He reads our magazines and really likes them. This man seemed very excited about your latest edition. He said he was very interested about the cliff with the dog and wanted to know if I could answer some questions for him. I told him that I knew you but had not been to Misty Mountain myself. He got more excited and told me of a place a few hours drive from where he lives. It is a small village up in the mountains and he says he has pictures of a cliff outside this village. He added that it was very mysterious, just like yours, as he has pictures of the same type mist over his cliff which also covers a valley. He said the pictures were identical to one in your magazine, including the dog. He sent me the pictures and he is right. I want to send them to you; this could be just a coincidence. What do you think?"

"Wow!" I said. I felt overwhelmed with curiosity, it gave me Goosebumps. "Have you ever been to this village? Have you ever heard of it?"

"No I have never been there or heard about it but plan to take a trip to this village to see it for myself." Mr. Chang replied.

"I want to join you! Can we go together?" I am still excited as I have so many plans running through my head. "I can bring all the pictures I have and we can compare and go see this cliff."

"I will wait for you if that is what you want. You let me know when you can get here and then I will make my arrangements with your schedule." Mr. Change said.

"Thanks Mr. Chang, I will call you in a few days. It has been great talking with you and I can't wait to meet you face to face." I said, and then we said our goodbyes and hung up the phone.

As I hung up the phone the four of us just sat quietly and looked at each other. After a few moments went by, Brittany got up; walked to the refrigerator, retrieved four beers and we all had a toast.

First thing the next morning as I was walking into the office, Lorrie was just getting off the phone. "Bob, I have just booked you a flight to Hong Kong. You leave Salt Lake tomorrow at 1:00 PM."

"Wow, that's fast, but perfect." I said, "I will call Mr. Chang and let him know when my plane arrives. Thanks Lorrie."

Brittany perked up and said, "Can I be in charge when you're gone?"

We all laughed at the way she said it.

"You will have to check with the other two partners I guess." I replied.

"Does that mean I am a partner now too? Yeah! That calls for another toast!" she said.

Sure, after we get done with what we need to today, another toast would be great. We worked all day and had our toast before leaving for the night. I went straight home and started packing. It took a while and I was pretty excited so didn't sleep well that night. The next morning we all met at the office again.

"I will drive you to the airport Bob. I'd like to stop and see my parents." Mark offered.

"Thanks Mark." I said, "But please don't say anything to them about this just yet. You can tell them I am going to China to visit an old friend but nothing about the real reason I'm going until I know just exactly what it is. I need all of you to keep a lid on this until we know the truth. Lorrie, would you please look after Star for me? If you take him up to the cliff in a few days maybe we can feel each-others presence, sounds corny but you just never know."

"We will take care of Star." Mark said, "We better get going. Don't want to miss this plane."

"Have a great trip Bob. Call us every day and bring back some gifts." Brittany said.

"Thanks guys, I am trying to not let myself get too excited but it is really hard not to. I am doing my best to just look at this as a vacation. I will find other good things about China to write about, I will call when I get to Hong Kong. If something important comes up here, feel free to call me. We will have a little party when I return. When I talked with Mr. Chang he suggested we take a train and that I would love the scenery. The ride will take about three days and we will make quite a few stops on the way so I can get some great pictures of the culture of his country. I will call you again when I reach the village. Mark, are you ready?" I asked.

We all had a group hug and Mark and I left for the airport.

Chapter III

I knew this was going to be a long flight so I decided to just read up on the material that Lorrie packed for me. There were a lot of things I wanted to see in China, the zoos especially. I was hoping Mr. Change could clear everything with the Chinese government and allow me to visit all the places I want to go to. I didn't think I was going to be able to get any sleep on the plane ride with everything going through my mind. I was very excited but I did manage to doze off for a couple hours. The man sitting next to me woke me up as the plane began to descend to our destination.

I was met at the gate by Mr. Chang.

"Bob, hello, it is so great to finally meet you face to face." Mr. Chang said.

"Hello Mr. Chang and yes our meeting has been long over due." I said.

"Please call me Le. Come, I will help you through customs. Then we will go to my office and discuss our plans for your visit. We can go over each others work." Le said.

"Thank you Le, if you don't mind I would first like to find a place to relax a bit and have a beer or two."

Le laughed, "Of course, your famous toast, I know the perfect place for that."

We stopped at a place along the way, had a beer and left for Le's office. It was very similar to mine back home. Le ordered us some food and had beer there already. We spent a few hours talking about where we would go during my visit. He had a village circled on his map and said that this is where we would go. It was located in western China. I told him where I wanted to go too and he was way ahead of me. There were three zoos on the way that we would stop at on our way to the village. He had already been to two of them himself. The third was the closest to the village. He mentioned some cities along the way that we would stop at as well. This trip would normally take a little more than a day but with all our stops we wouldn't actually reach the village until Monday, four days from now. This was going to be interesting to say the least. Le read me some of his stories. I couldn't believe how similar they were to the stories we write. Our writing styles are very simple; no huge words that people don't understand or know the meaning of. He agrees that people should be able write so all readers understand."

We talked for hours and had a few laughs. Le checked his phone messages while we were visiting and informed me that there was one for me. Mark had called so we called him back.

"Hello Mark." I said. "It has got to be pretty late there, is everything alright?"

"Hi Bob, everything is fine, well kind of fine. We are all here and wanted first to know that your flight went well, and since we hear your voice I guess it went fine." He gave a little chuckle. "Yes it is late here, I'm going to put Lorrie on and let her talk to you."

"Hi Bob." Lorrie said. "The reason we are here so late is that we wanted to make sure we got to speak to you before you left on your train ride. Earlier today we received a call about the mist. The call came from your friend in Mexico, Luis. He had a similar story to Mr. Chang's. He had received a phone call from a man who lives in a small mountain village in Peru. I have made arrangements to fly down there tomorrow. Mark and Brittany thought I should be the one to go since I speak Spanish fluently. I just wanted to check in with you and make sure this is okay."

"Wow! That is exciting news." I replied. "Of course it is okay with me. I'm glad you called to let me know. Mr. Chang and I are sitting here together with the same look on our faces. During my trip here I tried hard to focus realistically and not jump to any conclusions, so you need to do the same. Lorrie, I want you to consider this a vacation and try and focus on some other good stories that can come from your visit in Peru. Just talk to people, listen to what they think and feel. You did a great job on your last story, so I know you can do it. Please don't talk to anyone except Luis about me visiting China for the same reason. Also, ask Luis if he would like to come to Misty Mountain with you. I will be asking Le the same thing and he is nodding his head right now confirming that he will. I thing

Le and Luis can join us and we could all write a story together. You enjoy your trip and I will see you when I return."

"Thanks Bob." Lorrie said. "I was a little nervous at first but I feel better about it now that we have spoken. I think I know what you want. I will do my best."

"I know you will Lorrie." I replied. "Mark, there are a few thing I need you and Brittany to do. We are going to need extra supplies and I trust you in determining just how much. If anyone asks about Lorrie and I just tell them we are getting good things to write about from other countries. Brittany, please dig up every picture you have of the mist. Use your imagination and put a picture in your mind about three different countries, three different scenic views and three different dogs, one being Star of course. For now, all I am going to do is enjoy my trip. China has so many beautiful places to see."

"Hey Bob and Le, "Brittany shouted over the speaker phone, "If you have a beer handy, this is a great time for a toast, yes?"

"Yes it is, give us 5 minutes and then toast." I said.

"That must be Brittany." Le said, "I wish I could find someone like her to work with me."

"We could rent her out to you, but it will cost you." I laughed and added, "Better yet, whenever you have a story to send us, you can talk to her. You will meet her when we return to Misty Mountain. Mark, I would like you to check with your father about being in Misty Mountain when we return, I want him to meet Mr. Chang. But, again, don't tell him the reason for mine and Lorrie's trips. Okay?"

"I understand, I will have him meet us at the airport when you come back." Mark said.

"That will be great." I said. "Well our train is leaving here shortly, so we'll see you in a few days. Lorrie, you have good time and have some fun."

We hung up and Le said, "So Bob, looks like we will both be busy for quite some time. That Brittany sounds like a great person to talk to. I am looking forward to meeting her and the rest of your partners."

I laughed, "Yes, Brittany is a very nice girl, especially if you have a good sense of humor. We can talk more about this on the train. I just want to enjoy my trip and learn as much as I can about your country. I will have many questions to ask you about your land, farming, and I can't wait to see the animals in your zoos. I want to see and hear the good things we both love to write about."

"We have many good things here in my country and many different from your country. We can compare stories on the way. Has it been five minutes yet? Let's have our toast and head for the train Bob. This is going to be a great trip for you." Le said. We toasted and began our trip.

As the train was pulling out of the station I felt relaxed and just had a feeling that this was going to be comfortable ride. Le and I spoke about many things. Our first stop was in a City that had the first zoo on my list to visit. There were animals in there that I have never seen before and Le told me all about their originations. It was very interesting. We were there for about six hours before continuing on. All of our stops were right on schedule. The small towns were the ones Le most wanted me to see. They were very similar to small towns in America. The people were all so friendly, just like home. When we reached our destination we went to check into our hotel Le set up for us. After settling in, Le called the man who sent him the pictures of the mist and invited him to come to dinner with us at the hotel. He came right over. We had dinner and Le asked about the cliff and where it was located. The man said he reads all of Le's magazines but the picture itself was sent to him from a woman who lives in a village not far from here. He said he would take us there in the morning. We had dinner, a couple beers and then went to our rooms to get some sleep. I relaxed and went over some of my articles I brought with me. I planned on writing a story on the train ride back to Hong Kong.

The next morning we got in a jeep and started for a nearby mountain range. Le was translating to me what the man was saying. He said the trip wasn't far but the road was kind a rough so we would go slowly. We reached the village and once again, reservations were all set up for us thanks to Le. This little village reminded me in some way of Misty Mountain. It was in the mountains and had beautiful scenery. After we got settled, we drove up to a place which was similar, in a way, to the cliff in Misty Mountain. The scenery was different though. There were no mountains over looking the valley below, but they were more like hills. The valley below was completely different, but still very beautiful. There were two people there when we arrived. One was a woman with a dog. She introduced herself to us, her name was Kwan. She is the woman who sent the picture. We sat with her and Le translated back forth. He told her who I was and why were there. I was talking to Kwan about her dog and at the same time I had taken out some of the pictures of Star and I. I showed her the pictures of us at the cliff without the mist. She pulled out her pictures of her and her dog and showed me. I then spotted one of her pictures of her dog sitting on the edge of the cliff, looking out over the valley. The entire valley was covered with a mist. I asked her about it and she responded in the same way that everyone who has seen it responds. She didn't know. I asked her about her dog and she too feels that her dog feels something that we just cannot. She knows it is a good feeling and her dog knows it. I pulled out the pictures I brought with me and showed them to her. First I showed her some pictures of Star and explained that this is my dog. Then I showed her the ones of Star sitting at the edge of the cliff looking out over the mist. I couldn't believe the look on her face. It was like she couldn't believe what she was seeing. I smiled and filled her in on everything that I know about the mist. Le, Kwan and I sat there for a few hours talking. She too brings her dog up here as often as she can. I told her that I do the same thing with Star. I looked at the hills surrounding the valley and noticed a building on top of one of the nearby hills. I asked her what it was. Kwan told me that it was one of their religious places. I asked if I could go there and if there was anyone there that I could speak with. She said yes and that she could take us there. It wasn't very far so we left to drive there. There were some very friendly people there who greeted us. Le knew one of the men and introduced us. He invited us inside and offered us some water. I asked him about the mist as I showed him our pictures. He was surprised at what he saw too. I told him all about Misty Mountain and the history of the mist. He said it was very similar to the history of the mist here. He went on telling of how people came to this temple many years ago. They thought it was a message from god, so they established this temple as a sacred place. They maintained their beliefs for many years and tried to keep it a secret form everyone, but in time the new members realized that the mist should not be kept secret and that anything that makes you feel at peace with yourself should be shared with everyone.

It was very interesting listening to the man tell us about the mist, but even he, as wise as he was, could not tell us what the mist really is. He did not know that an identical mist existed in another country until I showed his the pictures of Misty Mountain. He had a smile on his face as we were saying our goodbyes. He asked us to please keep in touch with him and let him know everything we find out about the mist. We agreed and left to go back to the cliff. After a couple more hours, Kwan and her dog said good night. I asked her to join us the next day and spend some more time with us. She said she would meet us in the morning. We drove back to town and Le and I returned to our rooms. Once again I found it very hard to go to sleep.

The next day the three of us met at the cliff. We talked for hours with Le translating. We had a few laughs. Le ended the conversation by saying our train was going to be leaving in about three hours so we should start heading back. I told Kwan to keep in touch with Le so the three of us can tell each other about any new developments on the mists. She said she'd be glad to and came with us to the train station to say good bye. Before boarding, I gave her some of the pictures of Star and I and thanked her for the pictures she gave me of her and her dog. Le and I got on train and waved good bye as we pulled away.

"I'm going to call my office." Le said, "I want to make sure that all the arrangements have been made for my trip to the United States."

"Very good." I said. "I'm just going to over some of the articles I have collected while in your country. I have some great ideas for the good things about China I will write about for the next edition of my magazine."

"If you need any help with anything, just let me know." Le said.

"Thank you, I will." I said. "I have been doing a lot of thinking about the mist. Please listen to me for a moment and take some time to think about this yourself. This mist is new to you. Hearing some of the stories about it makes you feel something good. I am trying to prepare for the future and I really don't like what I see. Let me explain. I have seen this mist, Lorrie's grandfather has seen it, Kwan and our dogs have seen it and many others have too. Everyone has the same story about it. There is something good about it. You know how dogs are, they frighten easily but this mist some how makes them feel at peace. I just wish I knew more. In a way I am scared about what happens to us in the future. I feel as if I am putting my friends in harms way, now bear with me and I will try and make you understand. I have sent you some of our disrespect magazines and I have a feeling that there are going to be incidents where disrespect will be present a lot. Let me simplify this. There has been both good and evil in the world since the beginning of time. Fighting has become a way of life. There have been wars, people killing people for so many different reasons. It could be power, or greed and some reasons that don't even make sense to me like gang related killings. People kill other people just because they may be too different or they kill just to kill, they don't even need a reason. Fighting seems to have become a way of life for too many people. People grieve when their country goes to war, they want it to end. Police officers everywhere are constantly fighting crime and battling criminals. There are bar fights, domestic violence, fighting in sports, the list goes on and on. It all boils down to respect or lack of it. Do people even have a clue what respect is, and how powerful it could be. This story we're going to write about is only about the truth and good things. So you know that sometime there is going to be evil to balance the good that we will write about. Please Le, take some time and think about it. I really want your opinion on this."

"Do you really think something bad will come of this?" Le asked. "I agree with you in many ways but I will think about this for a while but for now let's get ourselves a beer, relax and enjoy our trip.

"Excellent idea Le." I agreed.

I did just that. I worked on my stories and at the same time I took time out to enjoy the scenery of China. The trip seemed shorter on the way back. After pulling into the station we had a few hours to kill so Le took me back to his office. I helped him gather his things before we headed to the airport. It took us a long time to get through customs. We boarded the plane and we were on our way back to L.A. The trip back would be much shorted than the trip there. I had a friend to talk with. We talked a lot with the other passengers and had a lot of laughs. Once the plane landed, we decided to go get breakfast because we had a three hour layover before getting on the next plane to Salt Lake. We landed around 11:00 A.M. Mark, Brittany and Frank were all there to meet us. Brittany seemed pretty excited, even more so than usual. We loaded our things into Frank's car and went back inside to wait for Lorrie's plane which wouldn't be landing until 3:00 P.M.

"You seem a little excited Brittany." I said. "I suppose you are waiting for someone to make a toast."

"Sounds good, but that's not the reason. I will wait and explain once Lorrie gets here, I can't wait! Now about that toast." Brittany replied.

Le laughed. "She is everything you said she was Bob. I'd like to make this toast to all of you, my new friends."

"None for me, I'm one of the drivers." Frank said. "The other driver will be along shortly. She is one of our young reporters. Don't worry though, she knows everything and will not do anything until you are ready Bob. She is a good friend of Mark's and will be helping with your story."

"Her name is Sheryl." Mark said. "As my dad said, Cheryl and I have been close friends for a long time. She will be the other driver. I will ride with her and we will try to get most of your luggage in Dads car so you all will be comfortable in the van. I know nothing will be discussed without me. Right Bob?"

"Right!"

It wasn't long before Lorrie's plane came in. We all met her at the gate and had a group hug. All the introductions were made and loaded up her luggage. We discussed the seating arrangements with Lorrie.

"Would it be okay to pick up a pizza and some beer on the way home?" Lorrie asked.

"What a great idea." I said

Brittany and Mark just laughed and I said, "What is so funny?"

"Oh nothing." Brittany said.

Before we go into the vehicles, Cheryl asked Mark if he would rather ride with his friends and he replied with a chuckle, "No, that's okay, because I know they won't discuss anything without me. Besides, Brittany has along list of questions to ask, so they won't have time."

Everyone else laughed as we got into the cars. We made our pizza and beer stop and headed home.

"Just what were you and Brittany laughing at back there?" asked Cheryl.

"I can tell you now." Mark said. "Tom and Barb are throwing a party with pizza and beer, we just didn't have the nerve to spoil the surprise."

As we pulled into Misty Mountain Mark motioned for us to follow him. So we followed him as he drove up to the cliff and parked the cars. As we got out of the vehicles, Mark said, "I couldn't think of a better place to have a group toast. Besides there is someone here who missed you."

Star came running up to me and licked my face. Tom was there with her and said, "I wanted to be in on this toast."

We just stayed for one beer and then Tom invited us all back to the bar. So we drove back into town and went to the bar. It was pretty packed except for two empty tables he had already reserved for us. We introduced Le and Luis to everyone and sat down.

I stood up. "Le and Luis do the same kind of work in their country as we do here. Some of the stories you have read actually came from them. I see you have pizza on the table over there." Mark and Brittany started laughing again. "Oh, now I know what you were laughing at back at the airport. Why didn't you tell us we would have pizza waiting for us?"

"We just didn't have the nerve to spoil the surprise." Brittany said, and continued on in a louder voice so everyone in the bar could hear, "Bob and Lorrie just had to stop for pizza and beer for the ride home."

Everyone in the bar got a kick out of that as the laughter filled the room.

"Le and Luis, I hope you are not too full because this pizza here is the best in the world, you have to try some." I said.

We spent the next few hours talking about our trips. Lorrie and Luis shared first, and then Le and I told them about our trip. We just discussed the great things we saw and nothing about the mist just yet. Mark made one last toast, "To new friends from around the world!"

Before we left I asked Tom and Barb to meet at the office the next morning. They said they would and we all said good night and went home. Le and Luis stayed at my house. They were so excited to be here that we couldn't go right to sleep so we stayed up for a couple hours and talked about what we would do during their stay. We decided that each of us have a story to write. I showed them their rooms and before turning in myself, I promised Star that I would take him to the cliff tomorrow.

The next morning we all met for breakfast and then headed to the office. Everyone was there that we asked. I could see that Lorrie would break soon if I didn't let her go first so I asked her to tell us about her trip.

"It has been so hard on me to hold back but I really wanted to share this with you all together." Lorrie began, "On my second night in Peru Luis and I saw the mist. I have some great pictures and the mist is everything and more than we have all heard about. It was so peaceful and I felt there had to be something more but I didn't know what. I got this feeling that my grandfather knew more but I never knew what it was."

Lorrie had tears in her eyes; I got up and gave her a hug. I was overjoyed that she got to see the mist. I knew Barb had to leave to open up the photo shop. I gathered all the pictures that we had and laid them out on the table. For the first time I saw the truth. All the pictures of the mist from three different countries were identical. I wanted Barb to see this. I told her that I would send Brittany over to the store when we were finished here. I told her and Brittany both that we would need something really special for the new cover. Barb left while saying she had something in mind already. I told Jim and Tom not to tell anyone just yet. "I know I can count on you both to keep this under your hat for a while, right guys?"

"You can count on us, Bob." Jim said as they left the office.

I looked at Tom and said, "You are going to have to quit throwing us big parties like you did last night. You and Barb have a baby on the way and these free parties just aren't necessary."

Brittany spoke up before Tom could reply, "Let me handle this big brother. Bob, we have talked about this, Tom and I, and all he is doing is showing his appreciation of a great friendship as well as the great business you have brought in. What you and your magazine have done for this town is more than you could ever know and it just keeps getting better and better. This is his way of saying thank you."

Tom added, "Sometimes it is very hard to believe that my little sister is a real blonde. Everything she said is true Bob, besides the tips you leave make up for everything. We will talk later. I have to stop at the photo shop before I go open up the bar. You can count on me to keep this under wraps for now; I won't say anything to anyone. See you all later."

"Wait a minute Tom, I need your help. Here is a list of people I like to talk with. Can you contact them and ask them to meet with us at the bar sometime Monday?" I said to Tom.

"Sure thing Bob, this won't be a problem at all. I will get right on it." Mark said as he left the office.

"Now there is a reason I wanted all of us here together." I said. "We have a fantastic story to write about. Le and Luis will be doing their own stories but I'm sure all three will be very similar. We had agreed that we would all use the same photos for all three. Cheryl, I am glad you are here. I would like you to do the story for the newspaper and work with Frank and Frank only. By no means print anything in the paper until you hear from me. It is imperative that our magazine be published first. Mark will call you when it is time. I also bought a globe, a big one for our office. It has a pole at the top of it where we will mount our first copy. Underneath it will be the words 'Peace Through Respect'. Now I'm going to take Star up to the cliff, does anyone want to join us?"

Everyone decided to go so we all left and headed up to the cliff. We sat around for a few hours and talked. Frank was the first to leave since he was returning to Salt Lake City tonight. Mark and Cheryl left shortly after and Tom and Brittany soon followed. Le, Luis, Lorrie and I stayed a while longer. We played with Star and talked about our countries and their animals. We all finally left to go home. The next morning Lorrie and I drove Luis and Le back to the airport in Salt Lake. We said good bye and started to return back home. On the way, Lorrie sensed that there was something on my mind. I found it difficult to explain to her what it was. I told her about my conversation with Le while I was in China.

"It's all about good and evil." I said. "Ever since I moved to Misty Mountain I have felt nothing but good and peaceful things. It was so easy to start my business there. Now I feel that all the good things that have happened will begin to equal out. I don't want that to happen to all the good people of Misty Mountain. Those people don't deserve it. I am going to try and do everything I can to keep Misty Mountain the safe and friendly town it has always been. I don't care what the cost is. I especially don't want to put my dearest friends in any jeopardy of all the disrespectable people that will be coming here. I know you don't understand but in a way if something bad happens I will feel responsible."

"Bob, we all love you very much." Lorrie said. "But you can count on us to back you all the way. We are a team and from the short time we have known each other, I can say this team you have put together is absolutely un-beatable."

"Thanks Lorrie," I said. "I do have a good feeling about all of you and I pray that this will be one time good can prevail over evil."

We drove into town and I dropped Lorrie off at her home then went to the bar. It was still early so they were pretty slow. Tom poured two beers and joined me.

"I have called everyone on the list you gave me and they all agreed to meet us here Monday afternoon before I open up." Tom said. "They all seemed a little concerned but agreed nonetheless. Some asked a lot of questions but I didn't answer.

"Thanks a lot Tom; I will explain everything on Monday." I said.

I finished my beer and went home. I spent most of the night just talking to Star. I know he doesn't understand but I think he just likes the attention he gets when I am talking to him. Sometimes I think he does understand. There are times I just relax and fantasize and dream about what people would wish for if they had one wish. Most of the time, I think, it would be for money because that is what it takes to survive in today's world. My wish would be to be able to communicate and be friends with every living thing on the planet. That wish would be priceless. I finally went to bed.

Sunday morning Star and I had breakfast at the diner and then went up to the cliff to spend the day alone. I wanted to write and let him play. I was just putting some final touches on story when Lorrie showed up to join us. We read each others stories for the first time and I was really impressed with her work. She always seemed to put a lot of heart in her work. She said she had something to tell me and began, "John is coming up here for a couple days. I know I have mentioned him to you before. He has been a close friend for a long time and grandfather really liked him. I never did tell you what he did. John teaches Indian culture at a college in New Mexico. I wanted to ask you if it would be alright if he joined us and saw what we do here."

"That would be great; I would really like to meet him." I said. "If you need any time off, just let me know."

"Oh no." Lorrie said. "He wants to pitch in and help us if that is okay with you."

I laughed and said, "You know there have been a lot of people asking if they can help. I keep telling them maybe later, but John is more than welcome to join us. Tomorrow is going to be a big day for us, so why don't we go home and get a good nights sleep.

We left for home. Star was worn out so we went straight to bed. The next morning we were all at the office early. We were very excited about getting started. Mark spent all weekend getting press settings just right for the new edition. I told him we would run this magazine for a long time and to keep track of the inventory. He was way ahead of me on this and had already contacted suppliers to insure we could have next day delivery for anything we may need. We began with the cover first. Brittany and Barb did a good job on this. It was divided into three sections with the words 'Peace Through Respect' at the top. Each section contained a picture of the three countries. Each one had a dog sitting on the edge of a cliff looking out over the mist. It was perfect. Just a couple hours later we started, John walked in. All the introductions were made and Lorrie took him into the back room and showed him what we did. I told them I had to leave for a while and go to the bar to meet with some people and I left.

When I got to the bar everyone I asked for was waiting there for me; Tom, Bill, the Real Estate Agent, Jim, the Sheriff and John the construction boss.

"Hi guys." I said. "You are all probably wondering why I asked you here. First of all, the reason I moved to Misty Mountain was because of the people. Everyone is so friendly and nice and made me feel right at home my first day here. I do not like disrespect and just didn't feel that here at all. Things may change though after the next edition of a magazine is out. I want us to be prepared for all the disrespectable people that may be coming here. I have a plan and will need all of your help. I think if we work together we can avoid the trouble that may be coming our way. First of all, Bill, there is a nice flat piece of land just 3 miles from town. I want to purchase this land to build a large hotel with about two hundred rooms. This will help keep them outside of town. We can talk more about this later. John, if it is okay with you, I want you to be in charge of the construction, and there is something else I will need you for which we can discuss later. Jim, what I would like from you is installing some cameras and microphones up on the cliff. They will need to be installed hidden from sight. They are not to be found until it is too late. I can explain the reason for this later too. We have plenty of time before the magazine will be done; we are taking our time on this one. I want to thank you all for your help on this and helping me protect this town from any trouble. After all, we do have Brittany on our side and I think we can have some fun with this." They all laughed and agreed to everything I said.

I left the bar and went back to the office. I called a meeting with everyone there. They all joined me and I explained to them what I just did at the bar.

"John, please don't say anything to anyone about this." I said.

"Don't worry about me Bob. Lorrie has told me all about you and the way you do things. You have my trust and respect." John replied.

"Now, how about a toast?" I said.

Brittany jumped from her chair and I thought she was going trip as sprinted toward the fridge. Everyone was laughing at her.

"We are starting Monday morning. Just to remind you, we won't rush into this. We will take our time, changing partners a lot and just have fun with it. We will stop on Friday mornings; have a group meeting and toast." I said to all.

A few weeks went by and we finally had enough magazines to make our first shipment. It seemed that my talk with them about taking our time had no effect on them at all. They were so enthusiastic about it they worked late hours but had fun the whole time. It's Friday morning again and we shut down for the weekend.

"The truck will be here this afternoon to pick up the magazines we have ready." I said.

"You have all worked so hard to get to this day and it is only the beginning. Mark, you can call Cheryl now and tell her to go ahead with the story but not to run it until Sunday. Also, I want you to take a copy of it over to this address. It's a surprise." I said.

Mark did what I asked and when he returned he was a little confused. "When did you do that Bob? Have any of you been at this place? Bob has a whole other building with a press and all the materials it takes to run a magazine!"

I explained to the group, "It is all part of my planning. I always did want to get a new press. You can use it to run your disrespect magazine. I just hope we won't need it to run our stories on the mist."

"You are beginning to scare me Bob." Said Brittany.

I just laughed. "Don't be scared Brittany. Let me try to explain. We all know that the government is going to get involved. You know it and I know it, they are going to try to make some kind of connection to our mist and the other two mists and try to control it. That is how governments work. When there is a connection of something between two countries that are so different, both countries will want control the whole thing. This is the reason I wanted everything kept under wraps. When our magazine hits the streets next week and the story is seen on TV, we will have billions of people who know the truth and it will be too late for the government to try to hide it from them. I think they will still try. We will be ready for them though. For now, let's take the weekend off and start up again on Monday. If you have some place to go or someone you would like to spend some time with, this will be a good time to do it. As for me, I'm going to spend the weekend with Star. First I think I will pay Tom a visit though, anyone else up for a beer?"

We closed up shop and went to the bar. It was kind of crowded for early afternoon. Most of the people there were tourists. As I looked around, I saw a familiar face sitting at one of the tables. It was Julie, a woman I used to date. I walked to her table and she stood up and gave me a hug. I introduced her to everyone. We were pretty close some years back but I left before things got too serious. There were no hard feelings between us; she always did have a great sense of humor.

Looking down at Star, Julie said, "So this is who you left me for. I don't blame you one bit, he is beautiful! Hi Star."

I noticed that some tourists had joined Lorrie and Brittany at their table. The tourists that were sitting there had all read the disrespect magazines. They really enjoyed them, as they had some stories of their own to tell.

"So, this is how you get your stories on disrespect." Julie said.

"Yep!" I replied, "Just a lot of people getting together in a friendly place and just letting it all out. Come on, let's join them and just listen." The conversation going at the time was about what we call noise pollution. "I can't wait to hear this one."

The man telling this story was middle aged, around 50 I would say. He said that when he was younger he used to party a lot. When the party started getting loud and bothering the neighbors, we would quiet it down. Someone would always step up and be happy to tell us when we were getting too loud. We responded with respect. That kind of thing just doesn't happen today. We used to care. The young generation of today, they don't care. People living in apartments or staying in a motel that there might be someone loud, they are scared to ask anyone to quiet it down for fear of some kind of retaliation. He continued to say that if his TV was a little loud and a neighbor knocked on the wall, his first response would be to turn it down and the next time he may run into his neighbor he would apologize. But people today, they would just ignore the request to tone it down or they will get mad and increase the volume. The people are morons that just don't care.

Another person got up and said, "You are so right. If there was just one person to say let's keep it down because we are disturbing the neighbors, just one person who says what they believe instead of just going along with the crowd, they may earn themselves a little respect!"

Julie smiled at me, "I see exactly what you mean now."

I answered back, "Now if Lorrie and Brittany can find a story there they will write and publish it in their magazine."

Julie and I lit a cigarette. A man sitting behind us began to speak his mind to everyone.

"I want everyone to know that I have been a non-smoker all my life and it has never bothered me to enter a restaurant where smoking is allowed. I think the smoking bans going on are ridiculous. It has gotten way out of hand. All those law makers who set these rules need to take heed of their advice. If the second hand smoke is harmful to them, then they need to quit driving. They need to walk everywhere because the cars they drive are more harmful to the atmosphere than a damn cigarette. The taxes they put on cigarettes too are ridiculous. If everyone stopped smoking then what will they tax? They get a lot of money to blow on their first class plane tickets directly form these taxes. Where is the intelligence? It really is getting out of hand. I have been bowling for 15 years with the same people. Three of the people on my team are smokers. It used to be a night I looked forward to. I got to know so many people from the league and we all loved this night. Some dick head decided to come along and made the law that banned smoking from establishments like this. We had 16 teams in our league every year. The year after it became non-smoking, we couldn't even form half that amount for teams. Three of my long time teammates never returned. The beer sales dropped drastically and rather than trying to fight a loosing battle, the owner had to sell the place. So I guess putting the working class out of business is what these law makers want."

Everyone was laughing and applauding the man. I mentioned to Julie that Lorrie and Brittany have some more articles to write about. The night finally ended. I asked Julie if she had a place to stay and she had plans to check into a hotel but I offered to let her stay with me and she accepted. I took her up to the cliff the next day and she left on Sunday.

The whole town of Misty Mountain was all a buzz on Sunday. Everyone was excited because they had read the newspaper. Cheryl's story was on the front page. She did a fantastic job with it. She kept it simple and true. Lorrie came over to my house and said she wanted to spend some time with me. John just left to go back to New Mexico and she didn't want to be alone. We took a walk up to the cliff. This time I did not go to my favorite spot and look out over the valley below. Instead we sat down and looked down on the town of Misty Mountain.

"It looks so peaceful, doesn't it?" I said. "I have a feeling that this week all that will change. Lorrie, are you ready for this?"

"We are all ready for this Bob." Lorrie said. "I just hope it is not as bad as you expect it to be. I know you are worried but everyone in town is excited and cannot wait. We are ready for anything. I really did like Julie, are you two considering getting back together?"

"We made no promises, but we did say that we would stay in touch." I said. "Julie and I had something special once. Not only is Julie a pretty lady but she is a very beautiful person. We both respected each other a lot. We really enjoyed our time together but the best part was that neither of us asked each other to be something we were not. We lived our lives and respected each other so much that when we were together, it made it even more precious. She knew I was leaving some day and she handled it very well, just like a beautiful person would. I think about her a lot and maybe someday we will be back together. For now though, we have we have our lives to lead. When one of us decides to make a commitment, then we will talk about it, until then, we will remain friends. What about you Lorrie? John seems like a great person too. It seems to me that your relationship is very similar to mine and Julie's. I hope someday you two can be together too."

"Yes, I hope that will happen too. And yes, our relationship is very similar to yours." Lorrie replied. "It is getting kind of late Bob, would you walk me home?"

We left and I walked her to her house. She gave me a hug and told me not to worry because we're going to have fun and added, "Besides, Brittany wouldn't have it any other way." We laughed and she went in so

I walked home. When I got home, I opened a beer, sat down and relaxed with Star.

Monday morning came and I walked to the office. Mark and Brittany already had the press running. There was a girl sitting at Brittany's desk.

"Hi Bob." Brittany said. "This is Susan, I call her Sue. She is going to help us out for a couple weeks. I have a feeling that we're going to get swarmed with phone calls. I don't want to be on the phone the whole time and not able to work and I know you wouldn't want that either. So Sue will help us out, is that okay?"

"Sure, welcome aboard Sue, glad to have you." I said.

Brittany ran over to her friend and gave her a hug as Sue said, "Does this mean we get to have a toast now?"

"Oh no, not another one!" I am thinking she will be fun to have around if she is like Brittany, so we all laughed and went on with our work.

The next couple days were very good for the people of Misty Mountain. Tourists flocked into town. Everyone was expecting this to happen and they were prepared. On Thursday morning, Jim came into the office. He had three men with him. One was an army officer and the other two were some kind of government officials. Brittany stopped them just inside the door and asked to the two men to take off their ties. She told them we have a strict dress code policy here. Jim told them they better do what she says and then introduced them to us.

"This is Colonel Smith of the United States Army and this is Professor Raymond and Professor Snyder. They are scientists and they work for the U.S. government." Jim said.

"Hello, nice to meet you." Col. Smith said. "We would like to take a look at this cliff and study it. We will be bringing in some equipment to do some tests."

"Well, welcome to Misty Mountain. We have been expecting you. I hope you can find something out that we haven't about this mysterious mist. We would like to know and let the millions of readers we have know as well." I told them.

Jim said to them, "Come on, I will show you the way to the cliff, we will walk up because all the tourists have filled up any parking there may be up there."

They left the office to walk up to the cliff. A few hours later, they returned and informed us they would be leaving and would be back in a few days. I asked Jim to stick around for a bit.

I asked Jim, "What did they do up there? What did they talk about?"

"I couldn't really hear what they were saying but they walked around and took a lot of notes." Jim answered.

"Alright, thanks Jim. Have you got everything ready?" I asked.

Jim relied confidently, "You bet Bob, we are ready."

Four days later Jim came into the office to inform us, "Here they come."

We all walked out the door and witnessed just exactly what I did not want to see. There were 3 big Army trucks and two government vehicles. Two of the army trucks had soldiers in them and the third was filled with equipment. The trucks stopped just outside our office and Col. Smith walked toward us.

I approached him and asked, "I thought you were just going to do a few tests. What's with all the soldiers?"

"It is just a matter of security while we do the tests, "Col. Smith answered, "It's really nothing at all."

"Nothing? You are coming into our friendly little town here with soldiers and weapons. Just the sight of you will cause problems; I hope you know what you are doing." I said.

Col. Smith replied, "I'm just following orders, if everyone cooperates there won't be any trouble at all. Now, can we ask you a few questions?"

"If you have questions about the mist, I suggest you read our magazines. Everything we know is written in them. It is the whole truth. We tell the truth, something you people should try once in while. If you have read our magazines, you would understand that there are only good things that have come from the mist so why do we need soldiers with weapons? You know the way to the cliff; do what you have to do. I understand you are following orders but please do us a favor and let us know if you do find anything out. I know you probably won't but if you do find out something, I know it will be something good and we would like to share it with our readers."

They all left on their way to the cliff. Later that evening Jim came into the office. He informed us that two of our kids drove up to the cliff and said it was all blocked off and no one can get up there. Jim and I took off for the cliff and were stopped. They wouldn't allow us to go any further. I asked them to please let us talk with Col. Smith.

As Col. Smith approached us I said, "You can't close the cliff off, why would you do this? No one is going to bother you, just do your tests and leave us alone please."

"I am sorry Bob, but I have my orders. We will complete our tests and be gone before you know it." The Colonel told us.

"This is just not right!" I said.

Jim took my arm, "Come on Bob, let's just go."

Walking back to the office I told Jim, "You know something? It is about time to find out what they are doing and saying. Let's go to the office and see how good your handy work is. We need to turn on the cameras, I will call John."

We were only in the office for a few minutes when Col. Smith walked in with Mr. Snyder. "We really don't want any trouble; we just want to ask a few questions."

Lorrie interrupted them, "When you were here before, Bob asked you to read our magazines. Everything we know is in there, the whole truth. I have seen this mist and I too had only good feelings about its presence. I have only known one person who might have known more, my grandfather. He is dead. There is one more who knows more than us though; maybe you would like to ask him your questions." She whistled and Star came running into the room. "This is Star; he knows more than we do, I could only wish I knew what he knows."

I told the men, "I really do hope your equipment can find us some answers and that you share your findings with us. If you will excuse us though, we do have work to do."

They left the office. I called John and told him to go ahead with what we had talked about. John and his men followed the plan. It took a few hours to move all his equipment but they got it done.

It only took a couple more hours before Col. Smith and a couple soldiers to come back to the office. "We need you to move that equipment off the road. You have it all blocked off and we cannot get any of our vehicles off the cliff." Col. Smith said.

John replied, "Oh, I'm sorry sir, the road was scheduled for repair and we had already informed the town that if anyone wanted to go up to the cliff during this time, they would have to walk. It should only take a few weeks. Just following orders."

Brittany had to speak her piece, "And please don't use the words, 'National Security,' Every time I hear those words it means that you are lying or covering up something."

John continued, "I gave my men a couple days off so if you can manage for two days, we will move everything. Please don't mess with any of my equipment; you might not like what happens."

Col. Smith and his soldiers left the office. Jim and I walked into the back room followed by Mark, Brittany and Lorrie. We sat down and watched on our cameras what was happening on the cliff. We heard the scientists ask Col. Smith if there was going to be any trouble. He answered them with, "That's why we're here." I asked Mark to call Frank because Frank has the cameras routed to his office as well so he can see everything we see. We told Frank to air this on the nightly news.

The next day Col. Smith came into the office and laid on the table some video equipment. It was our equipment, but not all of it. He stated to us, looking a little confused and said "This is not the cooperation we were hoping for. Our men have come into your town and have been treated very badly, why are you doing this?"

"Your men are coming here with weapons that you do not need." I told him. "It is scaring the hell out of people. Just how do you expect them to be treated? If they leave their weapons behind and act like human beings instead of soldiers, who, as you say, are just following orders, then they would be treated with respect. It is up to you, we really don't want to talk with you any more, and we want to speak to the person giving the orders."

The men left the office and I knew it wouldn't be long before the Col. would have some people there to move John's equipment. We all just went back to work. The fun stopped for a while, but with Brittany and Sue around, that wouldn't last for long. It was two days after the first airing of what happened on the cliff. Jim came in and said he received a call from one of the officers and that he was going to help us. Jim told him not do anything and to contact any other officers who agreed to help as well. Just a few hours after that we could see driving into town about seventy five vehicles. There were about a hundred people in all, protesters, people who like to start trouble. They drove up to where John had the road blocked and were met by Col. Smith and his men. Jim and I followed but stayed in the back of the crowd. We wanted to eves drop in on what the protesters were up to. I was right, they seemed to be led by one man, and all the others were just stupid enough to follow along. After a couple hours the crowd, was getting angry and we could see that Col. Smith and his men were preparing to take action against them. We decided to step in to help try avoiding any violence. Jim and I walked up to Col. Smith and stood by his side. Jim got on his radio and made a quick call. Within fifteen minutes there were a hundred and fifty police officers lining up between the two groups.

Jim asked them to quiet down as he pulled out some papers. "We received reports about a group heading this way, reports that you may be carrying weapons and maybe even drugs. We have search warrants to search all your vehicles."

The protesters didn't do anything violent, as they knew they were outnumbered. Half of them backed off and the other half got a little louder. There were twenty five arrests made with no violence. The rest left quietly and when they were all gone Jim and I were still standing along side Col. Smith and his men.

"You see Col, that none of Jim's men had to draw weapons at any time, while your men had them drawn and were ready to use them. I know your intentions are good but there is a difference. There is the military way and a way where good and peaceful people get together to make a stand. Our way works best here. That is why we were so upset to see all your troops and weapons enter our town."

"It seems that you were prepared for something like this." Col. Smith said. "By the way, did you really have search warrants for all of those vehicles?"

"Of course we did." I answered him, and continued, "We would not do anything illegal here. We are prepared for anything else that might happen here. You would be surprised at what we are prepared for and none of our plans contain any form of violence. If people want to protest, let them go to the white house to do it and leave our friendly town alone."

Jim and I walked back to my office. We went in the back room and joined Mark. He had already called his dad and the incident we just had will be aired on T.V. It has been a few days since we have had a toast so we had one now. Then we closed up the office and went to the bar. The people seemed more relaxed now than they did a few days earlier. Once again there was laughter. We still had a problem up on the cliff and we didn't know how long it was going to last. I took Star home and I could tell that he misses our little visits to the cliff.

The next day things were quiet. We got a lot of work done and heard nothing from the Col. And that made us all very curious as to what they were up to. The next morning, Col. Smith came into the office. It was just minutes after he came in when the phone rang.

"That call is for you." Col Smith said.

I picked up the phone and said hello. After I heard who it was calling me, I asked if I could put them on speaker phone. He said yes. I called everyone into the room and asked them to sit down. I put the phone on speaker.

"Mr. President, we are ready now." I said.

"Hello everyone." The President said, "First, I want to apologize for any inconvenience that we have caused you and your fine town. I have been watching everything that has been going on and have even taken the time to read all your material on this mist. I think we should have done that earlier. I have asked the Colonel to work quickly to remove all equipment, troops and weapons out of your town."

We all cheered as I motioned for Mark to make a call.

"Yes Mr. President, we will remove our equipment at once so they can do just that. We do apologize for the treatment of your soldiers and not being respectful to them. We just felt we were doing what we had to keep peace in Misty Mountain. The guns really made everyone nervous. We will treat them with the utmost respect as they depart though. They can have a place to shower and get a good meal at our diner. I would also like to take the colonel to the bar for a toast if that is okay with you. Can he be off duty?"

"Colonel Smith, you are officially off duty," said the president. "I have faith in you and trust that what you find out, you will let me know. I have been in contact with the people in China and they had the same trouble there. We have come to an agreement to work with us on this."

"That is good news." I said. "I know you have some very intelligent people working for you. Just remember there are others out there just as intelligent that may not have had the same opportunities as others. Just because someone doesn't have a college degree doesn't mean they are not smart. Experience speaks volumes; Lorrie's grandfather was one of those people. I'm sure you read about him. I think and hope that someday Lorrie will know the secret. I honestly am not sure anyone will ever know the secret to our mysterious mist but I do know it is a good thing. We can't rule anything out at this time, even religion. It could be an act of God but I personally don't believe that. I could be wrong but it is my gut feeling."

"That is a very interesting thing to say. I will keep that in mind. Once again I am sorry for the trouble your people endured and if there is anything we can do to help out in the future, let us know," said the president.

Brittany spoke up, "Mr. President, this is Brittany here," She paused, "Wow! I can't believe I am talking to the president. You mentioned that you read the magazines on the mist and I think that is great. I just want you to think about reading the one's we have written on disrespect as well. I have learned so much just listening to people and then putting it in writing. You could learn a lot. Some of the laws today are just something that a lot of people disagree with. The older generation didn't have so many restrictions and lived just fine. You will see what I am talking about when you read them."

"I will Brittany, thanks for the tip," replied the president. "Bob you got a fireball working for you there, she makes a lot of sense too. Brittany, if you ever want to leave Misty Mountain, you can come work for me."

"Did you all hear that? the president just offered me a job?" Yelled Brittany, "I will have to decline for now, I am staying right here in Misty Mountain where I know I am safe."

The president laughed and said, "I am going to have to let you go now, I am glad we got to talk."

"Alright Mr. President, if you ever want to take out from your busy schedule, you know you are welcome in Misty Mountain." I told him.

"I will keep that in mind, thanks."

I hung up the phone. We all felt so much better, left the office and went to the bar. We had a couple of beers and Col. Smith announced it was time for him to leave but we weren't letting him get away without joining us in a toast. So he did, and then shook our hands on his way out. He told us in the future, we can call him Steve. We all said goodbye to Steve.

Weeks went by. Things were getting back to normal but they would never be normal for me again. It was Labor Day weekend and we closed the office on Thursday and gave everyone an extra long weekend. Mark was going to spend the weekend with his family and Cheryl was joining him. Lorrie was going to see John. Brittany was staying home and having friends visit her. As for me, I just planned on spending time with Star. The town was full of tourists so the cliff would be packed so I knew we wouldn't be able to have it to ourselves like we used to.

Another month later we were sending out our last big shipment of the magazines. Then the work slowed down a little. Mark, Lorrie and Brittany were working on their magazine on the other press. I stopped in to check on them one day. A man came into their office. He was wearing a suit so Brittany did her thing. He also had a briefcase. He introduced himself and said he was from Wal-Mart and he had some business to discuss with me. I sat patiently and listened to him. I stopped him half way through his presentation. He was talking about them selling our magazines for us. I asked him how much he would charge in his stores for our magazines.

He didn't answer but kept talking about how much money they could make for us. I asked again how much he would charge for a copy. He then wrote down a figure and showed it to me. I said that we could not do business together. I told him that we make one dollar profit on them and our retailers make one dollar as well. We will not let our magazines be sold for more than that. You want to make a profit off of our hard work and I just will not let that happen. The man left.

It was the fall season and we had an early snow storm. Since the weather would start getting cold that meant fewer tourists. We stayed busy as our customer lists continued to grow. Once Christmas time came around we decided to have a party. We exchanged names and everyone got a nice gift. Brittany added another room to the photo store with all the comforts of home for Barb and the baby. Mark and Lorrie gave Brittany a desk. She was so excited and told them it was about time. I agreed, we are all partners now and everyone needs their own desk. Brittany, of course, ran to the fridge, got out the beers and we all toasted. It was a great time for everyone. Tom had bought the pizza business from the couple because they moved. To avoid the non-smoking laws he built another building at the back of the bar, not connected. The party ended and everyone went home. Lorrie invited me and Star to have dinner with her and John. We did and sat around to talk for while after eating.

"We had such a good time at the party." Lorrie said. "I completely forgot to mention that John is transferring to Salt Lake City this coming year. We will be able to spend a lot more time together and we are both so happy about that."

"Yes," John said, "I am looking forward to it. I have really grown to love this little town and want to be here when the secret of the mist is discovered."

"I hope that happens, and I hope it happens soon, we need something good in this world." I replied. I then said good night to them both and took Star home. The next week we had a little break in the weather so I was able to take Star up to the cliff. As I watched him play in the snow, I was doing a lot of thinking about the next year. I knew some things were going to change.

Chapter IV

It was a long winter in Misty Mountain this year, which in a way was good news for everyone. It gave everyone a chance to prepare for the upcoming tourist season. There was some very good news in town. Tom and Barb had a baby boy, Tom Jr. Brittany told Barb to take as much time off as she wanted and that she would take care of the photo store. While Barb was off, Brittany did a lot of touching up on the added room, so that it would be ready when Barb decided to come back to work.

Spring finally came and along with the nice weather, so did the tourists. It seemed like every day cars were backed up as far s we could see. This really caused a major problem.

John and his crew started on the motel. They figured that with good weather they could finish by the end of the year. There were a few good people of Misty Mountain that made small investments also. This did not bother me a bit, or the other investors, because it was a very good investment. Our magazines were bringing in a lot of money now.

We stayed very busy the rest of the year . All of the retailers would run out of our magazines in less than a week. I spoke to each one and assured them their orders will be shipped. They all understood. When they opened their account with us, I explained there may be times when something like this would happen. It wasn't just the magazine about the mist, but the dis-respect magazine sales really went up too. One thing I did make sure of was that we always have at least 1,000 copies of both magazines stored in the back room. These were for our local retailers. We wanted them to make a profit on this.

What we didn't know was that this was just the beginning. We received hundreds of phone calls from people claiming they have seen the mist.

Most of these calls were bogus. However, we received 6 calls from my friends around the world. They informed me of 6 other places on earth that the mist was seen. All of these sightings came from small towns or villages located near mountains. We didn't travel to any of these countries right away, but I knew that I would visit all of them in the near future.

The year ended with our Peace Thru Respect was the number 1 selling magazine of all time and the dis-respect magazine was in the top 10 and growing.

I really missed taking Star up to the cliff on a regular basis. Almost every time we went, it was so crowded with tourists we just went back home. We did manage to find time in the mornings for a couple hours. It wasn't until late fall when we could go to the cliff to relax and play. Star would play with the tourists and when he was done playing they would move out of the way so he could lay down in his favorite spot.

One morning I went up to the cliff and became very angry at what I saw. Trash was everywhere, beer cans everywhere and the odor was pungent. It took Jim only a couple days to post rules and laws around the cliff. He placed the cameras around the area again. Anyone caught littering would spend one night in jail and pay a $1,000.00 fine. There were harsher penalties for disorderly conduct and disturbing the peace. It seemed like every night, someone was arrested. Most of these parties took place late at night and were mostly young kids. The worst night was when a group of 10 kids were having a party. They were throwing beer cans over the cliff and making a mess. A car radio was blasting away with rap music. They were arrested and taken to jail. These kids were all from very wealthy families and thought a phone call to a lawyer would get them out of this. Their lawyers couldn't help. They all spent 2 weeks in jail and paid a $10,000.00 fine. The visitors showed a lot more respect to Misty Mountain after that episode.

I was thinking of just how stupid kids are now days. I was putting them all in this category, but quickly changed my mind. A couple local kids got some of their friends together and took turns going to the cliff every morning and cleaning the area. They were paid well for their good deed.

I started spending more time alone. I would go the cliff and look down on Misty Mountain. "Would this town ever be normal again?", I asked myself. I knew it never would. I felt responsible for this and began shutting people out of my life. One day, my three friends sat me down and talked to me. I told them how I felt. I was always thinking more of the bad things and stopped thinking of all the good things that have happened to me since moving to Misty Mountain. They assured me that Misty Mountain would survive. I thanked them for getting me on the right track.

The rest of the year went by quickly. I was spending every day in the office reading letters we received. Some were good and some were bad, and one really upset me. It made me start thinking of all the bad things again. The letter was from a family whose son went to a near-by cliff and jumped off. He committed suicide and this family blamed us. Once again, I felt responsible. Lorrie wrote to the family. We never heard from them again.

I knew that this would not be the only suicide committed and I was right. It's so very sad that people are taking the mist the wrong way. I started spending more time alone again. The only traveling I did, was to the zoo's. Being around the animals made me feel better. When I returned to Misty Mountain, I worked hard to get ahead. When this was accomplished, I announced at the Christmas party that it is now time to visit some of the countries where the mist has been seen. I asked them if they would like to go as teams to visit these countries and they thought that would be great. We had a long discussion on who wanted to go where. It was decided that Mark and Brittany are going to Africa. Mark and Lorrie will go to Australia. Lorrie and Brittany will go to Brazil.

I'm going to Germany with Brittany. Lorrie and I will go to Russia and Mark and I will go to Egypt. I always wondered why there no mist sightings in the middle-east. If anyone in the world needed something good to believe in, it would be there.

All of our trips completed, we had lots of stories to tell. I found the most interesting ones were about the animals. Winter arrived and we were working very hard with all the new material from our trips.

During the spring and summer, I would take Star to the cliff. He was getting old and slowing down. He would go lay in his favorite spot. Just before Thanksgiving, I took Star to the vet. The news was not good.. Star was really suffering and did not have long to live. The decision to put him to sleep was not easy. I spent the last night at home with him and it seemed like he knew. I cried for him and his head never left my chest. The next day I took Star to the vet and said good-bye. I walked up to the cliff and just sat there. As I looked out over the valley, my thoughts were only of my best friend is gone and I wished I knew what he knew about the mist. I got permission to bury Star on the cliff and put a fence around his grave. I know there was something very special about him, something we will never know.

Lorrie came to see me right before our Christmas party. She said, "You have been very sad lately. I know you miss Star, but I feel there is something more. We all want to try to help with these feelings you carry inside. We all love you very much and we will always be with you. So far, we have met every obstacle head-on and won. We are an un-beatable team and together we will survive anything. You taught us Respect. All of your ideas about good things are paying off."

"I know that my magazine is very popular, but you are responsible for the dis-respect magazine. If you guys keep this up, then someday we will have peace on earth. Thanks again, Lorrie for making me feel better. Now, lets get back to the Christmas party."

We walked back in the room just in time for the Christmas toasts. As always, our first toast was to Peace. Tom made his toast to Brittany for all she has done for him and Barb. My toast was to Star. The toasts were done and John stood up. He says, "I'm kinda new at this, so stay with me, I would like to start off the gift exchange." He pulled a small box out of his pocket and handed it to Lorrie…."Will you marry me?" John asked?

"Oh Yes!" Lorrie replied.

With all the excitement, no one noticed Mark and Brittany leave the room. They came back in and handed me a box.

"Merry Christmas." Brittany said.

I opened the box and the cutest little puppy was staring at me. I took her out of the box and held her close to me.

"What are you going to name her?" Mark asked.

I held this cute little golden retriever up in the air and looked for a few seconds and said, "You will be called Misty".

"Perfect!" Lorrie said. "This has been a perfect Christmas party for everyone."

I was hoping this party would never end. My new friend and I went home. I couldn't wait for a nice day to take Misty to the cliff. Our first trip, the ground was still covered with snow. Misty loved the snow and ran and played on the cliff. We didn't stay long.

Before we left, I picked her up and went over to Star's grave. I introduced her to this very special spot on the cliff.

About a year later, Misty was playing with the tourists at the cliff. I was talking to the visitors when I glanced over to Star's grave. Misty was laying beside the grave. I took many pictures of her. I felt she knew something about this spot. It's been a few years since the mist has been seen, so this was some kind of reminder for us. I stopped at the office on the way home and gave Brittany the pictures of Misty. When I went home, all I could do is just look at Misty and wonder.

Another year has gone by. I spent most of my time in the office reading letters. One letter got my full attention from a 10 year old girl. I let my 3 friends read it.

Dear Lorrie, Mark and Brittany,

I am 10 years old and my brother is 11. We are a very good family but mom and dad argue a lot. I love them both very much and they are very good parents. They argue and fight a lot now. It seems they hate each other and this bothers me and my brother a lot. I have read some of your magazines and I like the stories a lot, especially the ones about animals. I like the dogs the most. There is the word, respect, used a lot in your stories so I looked it up in the dictionary. I still don't understand it very much, but I think I have learned something about it by reading your other magazines. Mom and Dad seem to be arguing every day, so I finally did something about it. One day I told them to shut up and sit down. I told them that I love them both very much but they seem to hate each other and it bothers me and my brother a lot. We feel very sad for both of them. They tried to make me be quiet, but I wouldn't let them. I told them about how they taught us to always tell the truth, but when I hear them argue, there are some things said that are not true. I showed them an article in your magazine and made them read it. I told them that they need to do this. Let one speak and tell everything that is on their mind and let them finish without interruptions. Just listen, and then the other do the same. I told them at any time I heard them arguing, I would stop them. For awhile they did talk, but started to argue again. I told them to shut up again. I told them that they were bringing me and my brother into their conversations. I told them not to worry about us and that they needed to get a divorce. They were shocked at what I said. I told them that my brother and I love them both and that will never change. They are good parents but they should not live together because it's making everyone very sad. I told them they need to sit down and talk about this. By doing just that, they decided to divorce. Everything was taken care of without use of lawyers. It was good to see them just talking again. They talked to me about staying together, but I said, "No way!". Mom and Dad have been divorced for 2 years now. We are living with Mom but Dad can see us whenever he wants to. Mom and Dad have stayed in touch and are good friends again. It's so nice to see them talk and not argue. In a way, I feel that by them getting divorced brought us together as a family. Mom and Dad have read all your magazines I have learned a lot about respect in past 2 years. Even though we are not living together, respect has brought our family together.

Thank you, Annie

I read more letters, but none of them touched me more than Annie's.

It was later on that summer when we got a surprise visit from some very important people. We were all sitting in the office when Tom walked in. He asked us to turn on the TV. We turned to a local station in Salt Lake City. The news special showed Air Force One landing in Salt Lake City.

Brittany jumped up and exclaimed, "He's coming here to see us. This calls for a toast!"

We all laughed.

"I don't think he's here to see us." I said.

"Bob's right." Lorrie said. "If he comes up here, it's probably to see the cliff."

"Lorrie's right." I said. Besides, it's been a few years since we talked to him and no one has seen the mist for some time now. I hope he does come here. It would be an honor to meet him."

We decided to shut everything down and get ready for a visit from the president. We all had the same feeling. We knew he was coming here. We were right! A few hours later we could see government vehicles driving into town. The vehicles stopped at the edge of town and 4 men got out. We figured they must be security. The president and first lady got out of another vehicle with their dog. They started walking down the street, waving and shaking hands with the people of Misty Mountain. I smiled when I saw how they were dressed. All were wearing jeans and sweatshirts. As they got closer to the office, I recognized a familiar face. It was Col. Smith wearing a Nebraska sweatshirt.

"Hello Col. Smith. It's good to see you again." I said. "I like your sweatshirt."

We shook hands. "You can call me Steve. I'm retired from the Army and now work for the President. The town hasn't changed except for a few more tourists. You haven't got any surprises for us like the last time I was here?'

"No." I said laughing. "Nothing like that at all."

"Mr. President, let me introduce you to some of my friends. This is Bob, Mark, Lorrie and over there is Brittany. Be careful what you say in front of her."

We all laughed. "It's an honor to meet you, Mr. President." I shouted to Misty, "Come here girl."

Misty came running out of the office and ran right over to the President's dog. They hit it off right away.

The President and his wife stepped up on our porch and we all shook hands. He turned to wave at the crowd. There were about 20 reporters and photographers taking pictures and asking questions.

Lorrie asked if she could handle this.

"Go ahead." said the President. "I want to hear this."

Lorrie and Brittany stepped forward and put their arms in the air to quiet them down. Please, only one question at a time. "How many of you have read our magazines? I mean the ones about dis-respect. Not very many I see. Do any of you know how easy it is to answer a question when there is more than one person asking questions at the same time. No one is really listening."

Mark and Brittany went into the office and came back out carrying some boxes. Mark said, "We have some magazines here that you need to read. We will sell them to you at cost. Brittany, go ahead and do your thing."

I asked Brittany how she was doing. She said, "I've got $36.00. The pizza and beer are on me. Make sure you write this down, Lorrie. We do not want a visit from the I.R.S."

We laughed. Mark stepped forward. He said, "You there, young lady in the back. Could you please come up here. I noticed that when you were all asking questions, this young lady was silent all that time. I would like her to stay with us during the President's visit and let her and only her to write about this visit.."

We walked into the office. Mark hugged the young lady and gave her a kiss.

Mark says, "Mr. President, I want to introduce you to Cheryl. She is a special friend of mine and works for my Dad in Salt Lake City."

"No more surprises, huh?" asks Steve.

Jim walked in and shook hands with the President. "I know that you will probably be going up to the cliff, so I thought I might escort a couple of your men up there to make sure that everything is secure."

"Come here Misty." I said. "Take your new friend and go with Jim." Jim, two of the security guards and the 2 dogs left for the cliff. Brittany arrives with beer and pizza.

"Mr. President, would you like to walk or drive to the cliff?" I asked.

"I would love a good walk." The President replied. "Steve, could you bring the cars and follow us?"

The President, Lorrie and I walked, while Mark and Brittany rode with Steve. Jim had made room for parking and the picnic tables were ready. We sat and enjoyed our pizza.

The President said the pizza was the best he ever tasted.

We finished our pizza and Brittany stood up. "Mr. President, sir. This calls for a toast. You are probably not familiar with a tradition that Bob started when he moved here. Whenever something good happens, we always have a toast and this is a very good thing and deserves a toast."

"I would love to keep up with your tradition, but just one," replied the President.

The President, Steve and I walked over to the cliff and sat down.

"Mr. President, this fenced area is where Bob had Star buried. I was sorry to hear about Star, Bob. I know he was very special." Steve said.

"Thank you Steve," I said. I had brought along all the pictures we had. The President looked at the pictures of the mist from all the other countries, especially the ones with the dogs. We talked about the mist for awhile, then went back to the picnic table and ate more pizza. We didn't even notice the dogs had quit running around and playing.

"Would you look at that." Lorrie exclaimed.

We all looked over at the edge of the cliff. Both dogs were laying down by Star's grave looking out at the valley. Lorrie took out her camera and starting taking pictures.

"I've never seen my dog so calm before," the President said. "Now I'm starting to understand how you all feel about the mist. The next time I talk to my friends in China, I will tell them about this day."

"The last time I was here, I thought you were just being funny, but now I know you were very serious," Steve said.

"Well, I was being a little sarcastic, but it was the truth." I replied.

"I have learned something about respect today," the President said.

"I have always felt that anyone in my position should be respected, but I now know that there are a lot of things we do that don't deserve respect. Hopefully, someday we will have leaders from all over the world striving and working hard to earn total respect from everyone. I will do a lot of thinking about respect, but to be completely honest with all of you, someone in my position would be impossible to achieve. Maybe the answer to all of this is in the mist. I hope the secret of the mist comes to us soon. The people on this planet need a lot of help and now this mist gives us faith and hope."

The first lady has been very quiet all this time. She states, "I am going to make the mist my number one priority. I am going to talk with all the people who have witnessed the mist. I promise to help in any way I can."

"Mr. President, it's late and we should start heading back." Steve said.

"If you have any questions, please feel free to call me anytime," the President says.

"I have one question sir, Brittany said. "Just what is this Social Security? I don't understand it at all. I know you send us money when we get old. To me, it's like the government is babysitting my money. I don't need a babysitter to control my hard earned money. And another thing, just where does my money go if I die at 50 years old? Good question, huh? I had some papers drawn up and left with my lawyer. I know that it won't do much but I'm sure going to try. If I die before I reach 65, I do not want any of my relatives or my insurance company to pay for my funeral. Since Social Security has a lot of my money, I think they should be responsible for my funeral expenses. I know there are a lot of people who can't or will not prepare for their retirement, but there are more doing their own planning. I really don't need the Government taking my money, after all that's what taxes are for. What you need to do is check up on the 401K programs a lot of companies have today. You get to choose how much money you can invest and the company's put in a percentage. They can all go a step further with this. They can set it up so that a percentage of their money cannot be touched until retirement age and a certain percentage be available for emergencies. If done right, Social Security could be eliminated. Another thing about the 401K programs is that you can name a beneficiary. I want to choose where my money goes and not the government. I really don't want any of my money going to lazy people who reach retirement age. If these stupid lazy people don't care about their future, I say tough cow cookies!."

After a few seconds of silence, the President replied. "Brittany, if you ever want a job in Washington, just give me a call."

"No thanks! I like it here."

We all shook hands and watched as the President drove away.

We went back into the office. Lorrie and I just sat and looked to Brittany.

"I think this calls for a toast!" Lorrie yelled. "To Brittany!"

It took a few days for things to get back to normal.

It's now 2 years later before Christmas. We received word on our magazine sales. Our Peace Thru Respect was still number one and our disrespect magazine was now a very close second. The mist has not appeared anywhere in the world for quite some time now. Once again, I started spending more time alone and thinking back to the things that brought me to Misty Mountain. I never dreamed that just wanting to do something good would turn out this way. After spending weeks of thinking of my life, I came to a decision of what to do with the rest of my life. It was at our Christmas party when I decided to tell my friends. After the gift exchange, I stood up.

"Lorrie, Mark and Brittany, I can't tell you how I feel about you three. I can just say that I love you all very much and I have one more gift for you. As of the first of the year, you three will become equal partners."

"Wait a minute Bob, we are already equal partners." Lorrie stated.

"I know, but from now on everything will be divided among the three of you. You see, I've decided to retire."

"You can't quit on us now!" Mark exclaimed. "We need you!"

"It's not quite that kind of retirement," I replied. "I'm just retiring from the money part. I have enough money to live on the rest of my life. I will still be spending a lot of my time in the office and helping out. I do want to plan a trip to Africa. This is my home and I never want to leave it. Now, how about a group hug and a toast?"

Lorrie and Mark joined me, but Brittany just sat there with a very sad face. She stood and walked slowly towards us.

"I will join in on the hug, but I refuse to toast this," Brittany cries. "You said we only toast to good things. This is not good!"

"How about a toast to Bob?" Lorrie asks.

Brittany smiled and said "Okay!"

It was a long winter and I spent most of my time in the office reading letters and finding good stories to write about. I realized that all the letters were about people and none about animals. In all our magazines, not one was ever published without a good animal story. I pointed this out to my friends and asked them to never let this tradition end.

It was later that spring when John and Lorrie planned to get married. I was so touched when Lorrie asked me to give her away. She laughed when she said that I did not have to walk her down an aisle. They were going to be married on the cliff. This was all new to me since I've never been to a wedding.

Lorrie was beautiful in her tribal wedding attire. It was a beautiful wedding and the toasts went on what seemed like forever. It was time to throw the bouquet. This was funny because Brittany was pushed to the front so she would catch it. It didn't work out that way. Cheryl caught it and announced that she and Mark will be getting married soon.

The next year I traveled. I finally went to see Lake Tahoe and it was beautiful as I'd been told. Driving back home, I couldn't find a good radio station. I remember people always saying that rock 'n' roll will never die. Well, to me, it did die at a place called Woodstock in the 60's. People don't like it when I refer to that time of the beginning of drug music. The music got louder and the more noise, the more the kids loved it. The beautiful singing voices were almost gone, because the lead singers in bands just wanted to yell out words. There were a few good singing voices but all the up tempo of the bands made it hard to understand the words. I kept hoping that maybe someday, the slow beautiful music would return. Just when I thought the music couldn't get any worse, this thing called Rap came along. Not only is rock and roll dead, they are trying to put an end to all music. This is one change I will never adjust to. The kids love it, can understand it and hear the words. I guess that's why they all have their car radios operating full blast. I keep joking with my friends about investing money in hearing aids, because by the time they reach age 30, their eardrums will be gone.

On my way back to Misty Mountain, I decided to put a radio station in town. We would only play the old beautiful music. There will be one place in this beautiful world that people can come to and listen to music again.

The next year, things started to taper off a little. The tourist trade was still good, but not like it had been. Our magazine sales dropped a little, but our dis-respect magazine became more popular. A lot of our stories about good things, now comes from people who have made good things happen to them by using more respect. We still do articles about the mist and always have at least one animal story.

During the winter season, I decided to take a long trip and would be gone for awhile. I had everything packed and was ready to leave. We all gathered at the office for good-byes. I asked Lorrie to drive me to the airport. She asked me if I cared if John came along. I told her that would be fine with me. On the way to the airport, Lorrie said she was saving something as a surprise. They are going to have a baby. I gave her a hug and she cried.

"We are going to miss you." sobbed Lorrie.

"I'll be back," I said. "What's with these tears? It's not like I haven't done this before. I'll stay in touch and need to know how Misty is doing without me."

"I know that you will be back this time, but I have a feeling that someday you will leave and never come back," Lorrie cried, still hugging me.

"That will never happen." I replied. "There is only one place on earth I want to be and that is Misty Mountain with the people I love."

I boarded the plane, on my way to Washington D.C. to meet with the President. After a nice visit, I was off to Africa.

When I arrived in Africa, my friend Josh met me. He had arranged everything for me, as we had discussed my plans earlier. He also told me that he would accompany me the entire time I would be there. The entire trip would take at least 6 months, depending on me.

We began our journey. It took a day to reach our first destination. We only stopped in the cities for gas and supplies. The rich people of the cities did not interest me. I wanted to see the real people of Africa and learn how they survive.

We finally reached the wildlife preserve. We spent several days here, meeting with the people in charge of the preserve and just observing the beautiful animals they protect. My trip consisted of 3 more preserves to visit. We drove to a city located close to the Sahara desert. Two helicopters were waiting. They flew us over a small portion of the desert to a small city. I was amazed how vast this desert really was. We landed at a small city on the other side of the desert and continued to travel to the second wildlife preserve. We stayed about a week here. I was very exited to see the next one.

During this trip, I saw another part of Africa that I heard so much about. We passed through villages and people were starving. I will never forget the look on their faces as we gave them food. This was a very sad part of the trip. Later on, another very sad thing was witnessed.

While approaching the next preserve, we noticed police vehicles had the roads blocked that led into the jungle. The officers knew Josh and let us through. We reached the area where all the commotion was and I witnessed something that saddened me again. It made me angry, more than sad. There on the ground lay 6 elephants that had been killed by poachers and their tusks had been removed. I knew that poaching was a terrible crime here and the authorities are doing everything in their power to catch the poachers, but the killing of these beautiful animals continues. I mentioned to Josh that not only people doing the killing, but people who hire them should be given the death penalty. All of this is done for greed of man, people making money in the ivory business.

We left this tragic scene and continued on our way. We arrived at the wildlife preserve an hour later. I've always had a great deal of respect for employees of wildlife preserves. I was so disappointed when we arrived. The police arrested one of the workers who had worked for the preserve a few years. This man was caught giving information about locations of elephants and best times when they were alone and vulnerable to the poachers who would come to kill them.

I spent 2 weeks here studying the animals. This is a beautiful place. We also observed the animals in the wild. It was a savage place, animals killing each other for survival, but this is nature at work in its' cruelest way. So many animals must die so others may survive. Just where is the intelligence on this planet, I thought to myself. I see animals killing for survival, but humans, what do they kill for? Sometimes, no reason at all, but most of the time it's money. So, I believe the animals are far more intelligent than humans.

The last day at this preserve, Josh and I plan our next journey which will take us to the village where the mist has been seen. I plan to spend a long time there, visiting their cliff and talking to the people. We left the next morning. I t wasn't very far, only a couple hours.

We reached the village and it was exactly the way Mark and Brittany had described. This village was unlike the others I've seen. This village had lots of good ground to grow food and a plentiful supply of fresh water. Josh had informed the villagers in advance, so they had a place ready for us to stay. After meeting with the tribe leaders and having a good meal, Josh and I went to our hut and arranged pictures to show everyone. We went to the cliff the next morning and sat with the leaders of the village. Only two of them spoke English so they would translate to the others what we were talking about. One of the leaders who knew English had copies of all Josh's magazines. He would read the stories to the people. It wasn't long before the people of the village joined us on the cliff. We laid out the pictures in a manner where every one could see them. We noticed all the people pointing to one of the pictures and they were all laughing. I asked one of the leaders why they were laughing. He pointed to a picture of Mark, Lorrie, Brittany and myself. They were pointing at Brittany. The leader said Brittany was very funny and made everyone laugh and they did not want her to leave. I told Josh that I was going to have a talk with Brittany when I got back home.

Only half of the people have seen the mist. They didn't have pictures so when we presented our photos, they became confused. I picked out a picture of Star and passed it around. I told them this was my dog. Everyone was talking and when they finally quieted down, the leader said the mist in the pictures is exactly what they had seen.

Later that evening, Josh and I sat with the leaders. I told them that I really don't believe that the mist is a sign of God or any kind of religious thing at all. Whatever it is, they should not be frightened by it, because we do feel something very good from it.

We spent many weeks here and made new friends, not only human, but with their animals as well.

We decided it was time to leave and said our farewells and left on our journey. It took two weeks to reach the city. I thanked Josh for his hospitality and was on the plane back to the United States.

Mark was waiting for me in Salt Lake City. On the way home, I questioned Mark about Brittany's behavior during their trip to Africa.

"Don't even ask!" Mark replied.

Jokingly, I replied. "You are very lucky to be back home. They really wanted to keep Brittany."

We laughed all the way home. We went straight to the bar where everyone was waiting. I ate pizza and drank beer, while telling them about my trip. Misty never left my side. The next day, Misty and I spent the entire day on the cliff. My 3 friends joined me later and we talked for hours.

"Brittany, just what did you do when you went to Africa?" Lorrie asked.

"What do you mean?" Brittany asked. "Bob said to have fun and enjoy ourselves, so we did."

I spent more time in the office because Lorrie was about a month away from giving birth.

John and Lorrie invited me to their house for dinner. After the meal, we talked.

"Bob, there is something very important we would like to ask you." Lorrie said.

"We want to ask you if you would like to be Godfather to our son, Robert."

"I don't know what to say. I mean yes, it would be an honor. And just what made you come up with the name of Robert?" I asked.

Lorrie laughed. "When we discussed a name for our son, we decided on Robert right away. Total 100% agreement on that!"

Mark and Brittany arrived. "I hope we didn't miss out on the toast." Brittany said.

"No." Lorrie replied. "We were waiting for you."

"I was so deeply touched that I wasn't even thinking about a toast. Just when I think that nothing better can happen, something happens. I'm just so glad to have you around, Brittany, to remind us when it's time for a toast." I said.

We sat around and laughed and had a few toasts. I gave Lorrie a big hug, thanked her and headed for home. I sat down, had a beer with Misty's head in my lap. I looked at her and told she is going to have a new friend come into the world and to get ready to do a lot of babysitting. It took me a long time to get to sleep this night.

The next day at the office, I announced that my traveling days are over. I am going to stay home with the exception of trips to the cliff with Misty. I wanted to write one more story for the dis-respect magazine, but after some thinking it would end up being 2 stories. I tried to get caught up in the world of sports. I viewed highlights of some events and listened to the sports commentators. I never want to watch another sporting event again. Fighting is going on in every sport and teams resort to dirty tactics, trying to hurt key opponents from other teams and why? Because that is the only way they can secure a win. I can't stand the TV commentators because their heads are up their asses. Why can't they just tell it like it is. What is wrong with the truth? It makes me sick when someone will say something about the officials and get fined for it. All they did was tell the truth, telling it like it is.

Another couple years have passed and I find myself spending my time alone again. Star and I went to the cliff one night. I had the radio on and was enjoying the music.

Suddenly, the radio went dead for a second. This has happened before but tonight there was something very different about that moment of silence. We left the cliff and stopped by the bar. After a couple of beers, Tom came over and asked me if everything was all right.

"Everything is just fine." I answered.

"I was just wandering. You seem a little different tonight for some reason." Tom said.

Tom left and called my friends. They arrived a few minutes later.

"Tom called us and asked us to come over here to talk to you. He said you seemed bothered by something." Lorrie said.

"No, not really." I answered. "Misty and I just came from the cliff. I did a lot of thinking and you all know what I'm like when I do that." I added, "You are right. There has been something bothering me. We will get together in the morning to discuss it. For now, I think I'll head home to get some sleep." I turned on the radio when we got home. Once again a pause came in one of the songs, and I felt something different again. I finally fell asleep.

On my walk to the office, I felt different and I knew what I had to do. I entered the office and asked my friends to all sit down.

"You are all aware that for the past year, I've been going over all the stories written in the dis-respect magazine and reading the fan mail. We have had to knock a few people to get their attention. I would like you to write a good story on some of those articles. I have really put down the youth of today and actually called them stupid, but stop and think about it. We have all been there and done that. The world is changing every day.

Every generation has their own way of living. This time is so very special to the kids growing up. It's not easy for the older generation to adjust. When I was growing up, my parents hated my music and their parents hated their music. This has been going on forever and will continue. Adjusting to every generation is very difficult. Many of us can't do it. I don't like hearing an older person tell the youngsters that they need to respect their elders. Just being old does not deserve respect, it's something you earn.

The story I want you to do is on the life of a 60 year old. Not really the person, but what has happened in this world since that person was born. Let's go back 60 years and take a look. World War 2 and other wars starting. Look at how far technology has come since then. Go back another 60 years and you will find no automobiles and fighting was going on in the old west. Wars and fighting have been around forever. Now, let's look at today. Wars are still going on. We live in a world of computers and let them do most of our thinking for us. Let's look ahead 60 years and try to picture where your children will be. Seems to be a pretty good chance that all the oil this planet has to offer will be used up. If that happened today, many couldn't survive. I want you to find something good to write about, something special. Our readers like our stories. I hope all the resources that this planet has to offer will be used for something good, something that benefits all humankind and not use resources for weapons or any other kinds of destruction. Today, if you speak with the elders, very few do not want to think about the future. Write a story and give people hope for the future. I honestly believe that you are the only 3 people on this planet that can accomplish this task."

"Wow!" Mark said. "That is going to be very difficult."

" I think we can do it, but will need help." Lorrie added. "If only we knew more about the mist. The answer lies there."

"I believe you are right, Lorrie." I said. "Lorrie, I want to talk to you and John when we leave here today. It's very important."

As I walked Lorrie to her house, I explained to her what I wanted her to do. "Lorrie, tonight at about 10 o'clock, I need you and John to take me up to the cliff. Please don't ask why because I can't explain it. I just know I have to be there at that time.

I left Lorrie at her house and walked home. They arrived at the appointed time. We arrived at the cliff and walked to the edge of the cliff. The entire valley was covered by the mysterious mist. Misty just sat and looked. John was seeing this for the first time and the first time Lorrie has seen it here.

"It's exactly as everyone has reported," John said.

"Lorrie, I want you to think of your grandfather," I asked of her. Lorrie grabbed my hand and held it tightly. We looked at each other and not a word was spoken. I saw the tears in her eyes and after a few moments, we just smiled at each other. I kneeled down to where Misty was sitting and told her to go with John and Lorrie. She licked my face and obeyed. I then asked Lorrie and John if I could be left alone. Lorrie gave me a hug and went with John and Misty back to the car. John started to turn around, but Lorrie grabbed his arm to prevent him from turning around. They got in the car and Lorrie gave her husband a kiss and a big hug. She then whispered in his ear. "Bob now knows the secret of Misty Mountain."

Chapter V

When I finally opened my eyes, I found myself lying on a bed, in a small room. I sat up and looked around and as I looked, I began asking myself a lot of questions about my unfamiliar surroundings. The last thing I could remember was standing on the cliff in Misty Mountain looking out over the mist. I was very confused and very curious about my whereabouts. I just sat and looked around. There was nothing in this room except for the bed I was sitting on. There was a light coming from the ceiling, but no light fixtures. I noticed a door across the room. I went over and opened it and walked into another room. There was a man sitting at a table who smiled at me and said, "hello Bob. My name is Joseph. Please come over and sit. We have many things to talk about."

"Thank you, sir," I said as I went to the table and sat down.

"Call me Joseph," he said. "Here in our community, we are called by our first and only name. I can see that you are confused and very uncomfortable and probably have a lot of questions for me. Please be patient and I will try to ease your mind. You have not died and gone to Heaven. You are still on planet earth. Our island, which we call our community, is located in the Pacific ocean. As to how you were brought here has to do with the thing you call the mist. You will learn more about this later, that is, if you decide to stay. By no means are you a prisoner here. We can send you home at any time you wish, but we really hope you decide to stay with us and learn the reason you were brought here. There are 4 others from different countries here also. They are in other rooms going through this same orientation. You will meet these people later when we take a break.

A lady will be arriving soon to inform you of some very important things you need to know on your first day here. Her name is Jan.

A very attractive lady entered the room a few minutes later. She was probably in her mid 40's. She carried 2 trays and had some clothes with her that she laid out on the table.

"Hi Bob. My name is Jan and I'll return in a couple days to show you around. We have been waiting for this day for quite some time. Good-bye for now and I am so glad I finally met you," she said. Jan left the room.

"Bob, I want to specify one more time that at any time you decide to go back home, just say so. We want you and your new friends to spend one year with us to learn about our community and our way of life. It's very important that you learn about our plans, not only to us, but to everyone on this planet. It will take one year and we will meet again in 6 months to go into more details. For now, we will concentrate on making your visit comfortable and pleasant. Before we get to the items on the table, I will instruct you on our use of restrooms." We walked out back and he led me to a little building that looked like an outhouse.

Joseph continued, "This will seem strange at first, but you will get used to it. As you can see, there is a place to sit, you will always need to sit down. You will see a flow of water underneath. The water has a chemical in it that neutralizes everything and within minutes the water will be fresh and safe to drink. You will notice 2 buttons on the wall. When you are finished, you push the top button."

Joseph pushed the top button and a panel slid out from the wall and water started spraying upwards. When the spray stops, just push the bottom button and the panels will slide back into the wall. You will be completely cleansed and don't even have to dry off. You will adjust quickly. The canal below runs from one ocean to the other end and at no time will you ever smell the odor of sewage. You will learn more about the chemicals we use here later. Every chemical used here is harmless to the human body. Let's go back inside and talk about the clothes and the items on the trays that Jan delivered.

Joseph handed me the clothes. I went into another room to put them on. They felt very silky, but were not silk. I've never seen material like this. The shoes were soft and comfortable. I returned to the other room and sat down. "These are very comfortable" I commented to Joseph. "They are probably very expensive."

Joseph smiled at me and answered, "They probably are where you come from, but we don't have money here. There is no value on anything in our community. We all work together and share everything here. For example, our doctors take care of anyone needing medical help. In return, they received food and housing. The people who do our construction receive food, housing and medical for their services. The people who grow our food receive housing and medical also. We all help each other all the time to make sure that we have everything we need to live a very good life. I know that without money where you come from makes it impossible to exist. All the people need to learn is how to take the greed out of the money and work together, but the life as it is on this planet makes this simple little thing seem impossible."

"I know what you mean, Joseph and I can't wait to see your island and your way of life here."

"Now, the next thing I want to talk about is about our food and water. This first tray contains food items. You will notice the items are shaped like crackers. Each one contains all the essential ingredients the body needs to survive. What you know as artificial flavoring is added to each cracker. They are numbered to make it easy for you to decide what to eat. There is a book beside the tray that you may read to help you identify the crackers. We have learned a little about what you like to eat, so I suggest 47B. Look in the book and see what 47B is. The number 47 represents eggs, 47A is fried eggs and 47B is scrambled eggs. Go ahead and take a bite."

I took a bite and chewed it. The cracker tasted just like scrambled eggs. "This is very good." I exclaimed.

Joseph continued, "If you notice that there are only 15 different items on this tray which are your favorite kinds of food. I noticed several crackers numbered 1137. Now, let's look on the other tray. Pick up the plastic container by the tray and bring it over here to this wall with the 2 buttons, a red one and a blue one. The red one is for hot water and the blue one is for cold water. If you want coffee, push the red button or if you prefer milk or water, push the blue button. I held the glass under the faucet and pushed the blue button. It only gave me a half glassful. "Did I do this right?" I asked. My glass is only half full.

Joseph smiled at me again. "Yes, you did it right. You see, Bob, that you will only receive half glass each time. All of our pills are made for that amount of water. Our food and water are our number 1 priority and we do not waste any. You are free to eat and drink as much as you like, though."

"Is that yellow pill what I think it is?" I asked.

Joseph smiled again. "Yes it is and it contains alcohol, just like the beer you enjoyed at home. Now, open the small box laying there next to the tray. This box contained cigarettes about half the size of a normal one and a very short filter.

"Go ahead and light one. I don't smoke but many people here do. Don't worry about the second hand smoke, because it is not a problem here. Just exhale up in the air. Our ventilation system throughout the island makes smoke go straight up into the air. No one will ever experience second hand smoke here. When you are finished, just drop it down this tube in the wall. It will go into the canal and will be completely dissolved within minutes. Now, let's go outside and give you the first sight of a part of our community."

We walked out the door and were met by 8 of the residents who came up to me and welcomed me to the community. I recognized a familiar face among another group of 4. It was Kwan, a lady I met in China. I was then introduced to the other 3.

"Bob, this is Ivan from Russia, Sanchez from Brazil and Sarah from Africa. Sarah is the only one that speaks English, but you may speak to the others with our help, because we are fluent in all languages."

We all looked at our new surroundings as our mentors told us a little about their community. Joseph told me of the main street which runs across the entire island. It looked more like and airport runway than a street. It was at least 200 feet across. We began to attract a crowd. They waved and welcomed us to their home. Joseph informed me that everyone here has been waiting for us for quite some time. We walked on while Joseph continued with facts about the street and the buildings that lined both sides.

"If you will all come with me, I'll take you to a place where you will be able to see most of our community." Joseph said.

Joseph led us to a room with a large platform surrounded by glass or something similar to glass. We were ordered to get on the platform and sit in the 10 chairs connected to the platform. We sat and felt the glass. It was not glass, but some form of plastic. Joseph pushed a button and the platform began to rise slowly. The ceiling opened up.

"We are 100 feet off the ground now," Joseph said. " Feel free to get up and walk around. Don't be frightened because you are very safe here. Look down on the street and see many people waving. Feel free to wave back. You can almost see the ocean in the distance. You can see some of our transportation devices below. Jan will explain about them and many other things when she shows you around the island. The others are being told the same in their language. I know you are curious about all the buildings lining both sides of the street. Jan will take you to each of the buildings and explain what we do in them. Behind these buildings in the distance, you can see many houses. There are different kinds of living quarters in each section. One section consists of tee pees. Native Americas live there. That will be a section where you will live. Next to that section is where Sanchez will live and further down where you see a lot more trees that make up a jungle is where Sarah will live. Ivan and Kwan will live on the other side of the street. Jan will provide a map, but in time you will learn where everything is.

We stayed for a few hours and since Sarah spoke English, I visited with her most of the time. I learned that we all had a lot in common. Sarah spent most of her life traveling around Africa and working in the game preserves. Sanchez traveled through South America, Central America and Mexico. Kwan didn't travel much, but read a lot of books and studied animal life in China through her computer. Ivan also traveled a lot throughout Russia, working mostly in the zoos. We all loved animals, we all lived alone, and we all traveled. We all knew that our disappearances would not cause suspicion from anyone.

We finally descended to the ground floor and walked outside.

Joseph talked to me again. "There are many things we want you to learn while you are here if you decide to stay. You are going to learn many things from Jan that you won't understand, but, in time they will make sense to you. What I'm trying to say here is that we are far more intelligent than anyone on the planet and in a year, you will know more than you could ever dream of."

"Showers are next on our agenda for today." Joseph continued, "Over here is one of our little toys we have a lot of fun with. I think you would say it resembles a golf cart. They seat 2 people and there are 5 of them here on the island. We will use these to get to the showers which are about 3 miles away. Most of us enjoy the walk and find it relaxing."

We arrived at the shower. Water fell from a small cliff about 12 feet high. The small pond was about 3 foot deep. A few people were standing under the waterfall and some were just laying in the pond.

" They are waving at us to come and join them." Joseph said. "As you can see, after they shower some like to lay and relax in the water. Only 5 minutes under the waterfall will completely cleanse you and your clothing. Once a day here is all you need , but feel free to come as often as you want."

We all walked over to the pond and stepped in and stood under the waterfall for about 5 minutes. It was so refreshing and smelled so good, but it was an odor I have never smelled before, just like the restroom episode earlier that day. The people were all pleased to finally get to us. We stepped out of the pond and within 5 minutes our bodies and clothing were completely dry.

Joseph noticed the look on our faces when we felt our clothes. He informed us that we would learn more about their water later on.

We headed for our building. Someone had put chairs outside for us. There was also a table with food and pills. We all sat around and with help from translators, enjoyed a good conversation and laughed a lot. People continued to stop and say hello and expressing their welcomes. I ate some snacks and all were very tasty and I was on my third yellow pill when I stood up.

"I know this is our first day here and I am still very confused as to why we were brought here. I do have a feeling that it is something good. I have a tradition at home and it's toasting to good things. I would like for you to join me in a toast to our new friends."

Joseph stood to speak to us. "The sun will be setting soon. This is our favorite time of the day, so just relax and enjoy the next few hours.

As the sun was setting, the leaves in the trees started to sway. The wind was picking up but was a gentle breeze on the ground. The wind picked up and I could hear a sound coming from the trees. It was the most beautiful sound I have ever heard. It was not loud and I questioned Joseph about this.

"We have created a wind tunnel that blows thought the trees every night at this time. The music is heard throughout the island. We have installed different devices that are similar to the wind instruments you make music with, in every tree. This music remains at the volume you hear now and will continue for at least 3 more hours and then begins to disappear as the wind slows down. The music and gentle breeze relaxes our animals and gives them a sense of peace which puts them to sleep. When the music ends, all the people go home to bed except the ones who are working. That brings me to the most important thing you must do every night. There will be a pill in your room each night and you must take it. This must be done by everyone here and I cannot express the importance of this enough."

We all got up and went inside the building. Joseph walked me to my room and when I entered, I noticed a table had been placed there. There was a tray with some snacks and a little white pill shaped differently from all the other pills.

"Bob, I know you are debating whether to take the pill. It is harmless to you and it's not a drug of any kind. Think of it as a sleeping pill. In 6 months time, I can tell you all about it. If at any time you decide to quit taking the pill, you will be sent back home and will not remember anything about this island. I really hope this will not happen."

Joseph smiled again and left the room. I sat on the bed for a few minutes and thought about what I had experienced today. I thought about my friends back home. I stared at this pill, and thought I've never done drugs in my life. I then shifted my attention to the mist and how it made me feel. There is definitely something good here. I dropped the pill in the glass, drank it and laid down to go to sleep.

I woke up feeling very good after the best nights sleep I've ever had. I went into the other room where Joseph was waiting.

"Good morning Bob." Joseph said. "How about some breakfast before we get started today?"

I sat down and looked through the book. I selected my crackers and ate. I took my glass and got my half glass of hot water and dropped a pill in it. I had eggs, bacon, toast and coffee with cream and sugar. Joseph asked if I would like to start the day with a walk to the waterfall. He reminded me that we did not have to take a shower and only one a day was sufficient. I told him I would love to take the walk and expressed how very good my breakfast tasted. I then excused myself to go out back. When I returned I told Joseph that I could get used to this.

Joseph laughed. "Come on, let's go join the others out front as they have all agreed to a walk to the waterfall."

We joined the others and learned that everyone had taken the pill last night.

"Today, I will tell you about our Island." Joseph started. "When I leave you today, you will not see me again for 6 months. After that time, you will have become very knowledgeable about our Island and our community. We really don't know what came first, our Island or the 6 continents that make up the land formations on earth. Our animals, land and the things that grow here make our Island unique. We will turn here and take this road to the waterfall. This road is much smaller. These smaller roads divide the sections that you observed from the platform yesterday. The road we are on now is where you will be living and Sanchez will be living in a section across the street. On the left, you will find every kind of food items, flowers and trees like the ones in the United States. You will also see the animals that reside there. The other side of the street has the environments of Mexico and South America. I want to take this time to clarify the different animals. All are domesticated and are pets to our people. Everyone knows that feeding the pets is number 1 priority. Every animal depends on us for food. We do not have rats, mosquitoes or any kind of disease carrying insects that could harm us or make us ill. The bees here pollinate our flowers and no one has ever been stung. There are some insects that live underground that enrich our soil. We are normal human beings and do not live long lives. There is not a fountain of youth to keep us young. Some die from natural causes and some have passed away with cancer and heart failure. Look at the eagles up in the sky. They are not predators like the ones where you come from. They are our pets and depend on us for their food.

We stopped in the middle of the farming area. Joseph started explaining, "T he farming areas are the most important part of each section and take up a lot of room. As you can see, Bob, the larger fields are where we grow the main parts of our food supply, like wheat and oats and grains that a body needs. The smaller areas are for food. Just one of these corn stalks will supply us with the taste of corn for 3 months. Two fruit trees give us enough fruit to last a year. We extract some of the juices to make the artificial flavoring for our crackers and pills. I think you get the idea. Each cracker has 275 ingredients and each pill has 72 ingredients. You will see how this works when Jan takes you through our factories.

"I don't understand, Joseph." I interrupted. " With all this technology, why can't you help the starving people of the world?"

"Let me try to explain", answered Joseph. "It was thousands of years ago when people arrived here. They had different colored skin and spoke different languages. Within a short time, they learned to communicate and worked together to make it the community it is today. They decided to divide the Island into sections and each race lived in their section and were very unaware of how the rest of the world was. I really don't know how they knew, but they did. One day, a ship was spotted and they were very curious. They gathered for a meeting and made a pact no one was to leave the island and decided they did not want outside visitors. This didn't last long as they became too curious. Another meeting was called and they selected a handful of people to visit other land masses of the planet. They were instructed not to interfere with the way things were done in these new environments, only take notes to bring back to the Island.

During these talks, scientists were busy developing a machine that would allow them to travel under water. The machine was small and fast and could travel up to 80 mph. Radar and sonar devices were installed. They were far more advanced than anything you have today. They have improved on these devices over the years and by using them, no one on the planet can ever see our Island or detect anything that goes on here. Other scientists developed a cloud like substance that would cover the Island completely. This is the same mist that you have seen. With the different environments and the elements, we are able to make this mist appear and disappear anytime we choose. Bob, you and your friends have discovered all 9 locations where the mist appears, but no one without our help will ever know the reason they exist. The machines were finally ready and the 5 travelers were selected to go with the 5 machines. To this day, we don't know how the 5 travelers knew which way to go. They left in 5 different directions. Somehow they knew, like the black man left in the direction of Africa, Asian went towards Asia and the white traveler went to Europe. How they knew which race lived where is still a great mystery to us. These travelers were going to be gone about a year. After their returns a year later, the people were very excited to hear what they had to say. Each report and stories were very similar. It seemed every race wanted power and wanted to rule the world. Wars and fighting were everywhere. Wars were started over skin color and the speaking of different languages. The Island people met again and discussed the situations on the planet outside their Island. They all agreed to remain on the Island. It was another 50 years before sending the next group of travelers to see if any progress had been made. They only stayed 6 months this time. The reports and stories had not changed much. There seemed to be some progress to become more civilized but, it was still a very violent place to live. They decided to send travelers every 10 years, but the reports were always the same. It wasn't until about 100 years ago that we sent a traveler to a land you call the United States. This traveler came back with different stories. People came from all over the world to live there in peace, but this was not to be. Hatred and fighting existed because they were different. He also reported more progress and many inventions being made and the United States was becoming more powerful than any of the other countries. These people were discovering many things the planet had to offer, but they were using the elements for all the wrong reasons. When a source of energy was found, they would make weapons out of it. The world is still a very violent place to live. If only the people would use the elements on this planet for good things. It's not only the weapons today that make a country powerful, but money and greed and the people that have it. Now, you have asked me why we don't help them. If the people of the world knew what we know, the world would turn to chaos. We can't let that happen. I really don't want to discourage you in any way, Bob, about staying here with us. I know that in time you will find all the love and the respect you have dreamed of. Every day you spend here will be beneficial to your total understanding. Tomorrow, you will meet with Jan and she will show you everything on the Island. This will take about 2 months. After that orientation is done, you will be free to go anywhere. Everyone on the Island has responsibilities to see that everything gets done, but you and your friends will have none."

As we approached the building, Joseph said that we would sit outside as we did the night before. Food and pills were on the table. The other four mentors shook hands with their new friends and said good-bye. Joseph said he would stay with us tonight and help us communicate. We really didn't have much time to talk as thousands of people stopped by to say hello. After the people welcomed us, they went across the street to a very large building. It was huge, at least as big as a football field. Joseph told us this was their entertainment building and that Jan would be taking me there tomorrow night.

I really didn't say much tonight, just observed and listened. I tried to read the faces of my new friends to see their reactions of what they had learned today. I was just trying to relax and sip on my beer. The sun was setting and the leaves began to sway and the music began. Joseph was leaving and told me he would be back in 6 months. We all went to our rooms. I didn't go to sleep right away tonight. I just sat, had a few more beers and thought about my friends at home. It's only been 2 days and I missed Lorrie, Brittany and Mark, but most of all I really missed Misty. Whenever I was alone and did a lot of thinking, Misty was always there to comfort me. I looked over at the little white pill a few minutes before taking it and going to sleep.

I awoke, feeling very refreshed again. I went into the other room and Jan was there.

"Good morning Bob!" greeted Jan.

"Good morning Jan. Just what is in that pill that makes me feel so good in the mornings?" I asked.

"I'll explain that to you later," she replied.

"It seems that whenever I ask a question, you always say later." I said.

Jan laughed. "I guess it does sound like we are holding things back from you, but please be patient and all your questions will be answered."

I smiled back at her. "You know Jan, I almost did not take the pill last night"

"I'm glad that you did." Jan said. "I understand just how hard all this is for you and I think that each and every day you are here, things will become easier for you to understand. Why don't you have some breakfast and then I'll take you to your new home."

As we walked through the housing part of my section, I couldn't help to notice that all the houses were different colors. I haven't seen colors like this since I saw a Dick Tracy movie. There were no sidewalks, only paths. The paths were wide enough for the small transportation machines. All paths led to the streets that divide the sections. All lawns were green and flowers and trees everywhere.

We stopped in front of a blue house. "I hope you like blue," Jan said. "This will be your home for as long as you are here."

Jan opened the door and I followed her inside. I saw one large room that seemed so empty. There was a bed, nice comfortable chair, and a nice size table extending from a wall. The table has 2 built in trays. The large tray was for my food, smaller one for my pills. The books containing food and drink items were near the trays. A map of the Island lay on the table and some paper and pencils. The wall beside the table was the faucet where I would get my water from. There were no windows, but the room was very well lit from light coming in from the ceiling as in the other building. The door at the back of the room was my bathroom. There is no radio, TV, stove or sink and I thought how can I live here? "This puts a whole new meaning to the comforts of home!" I uttered.

Jan laughed. "I think I know what you mean, but this is the way we all live here." All of our houses on the island are constructed for sleep and privacy. Let me show you something. I'm going outside and will walk around the house speaking very loudly."

Jan went out and returned after a few minutes. "Did you hear anything?" she asked.

"I didn't hear a thing." I answered

"All the houses are constructed with a soundproof material. I know you have sound proof rooms at home but they are very expensive. Some day, someone will come up with the technology to build anything with this type of material." Jan informed me.

"Do you have any idea of how much money could be made with this technology?" I asked. "I mean if just apartment complexes, motels and hotels used this, you could make a fortune!"

"We all know of the human race and their greed." Jan quipped. To tell the truth, Bob it would be very much cheaper to build buildings with our material than it does for you to build these soundproof rooms. Any building could be constructed faster and cheaper, and knowing how to do this and since it would be a new concept, they would charge 5 times more. The only people that could afford to do this is the wealthy and that is just not fair!"

"That is exactly how it is at home." I said.

"Now come outside and I will tell you more about privacy."

We went into my front yard and Jan pointed to a chair on my porch. "If you like to sit outside, as many of us do, you may sit on the porch or your lawn.. If you are on the porch, you are telling everyone you do not wish to be disturbed. If you are on the lawn, they will join you to talk, because they all want to talk to you. Now, let's go back inside and I'll tell you one more thing before we go to the farming area."

"Privacy is very important, but people at home have no respect for the privacy of their neighbors any more. You will find some that will disagree with me , but why does everyone have to carry a cell phone with them all the time?" I asked. "They are on the phone constantly talking about nothing, just talking!"

Jan chuckled. "I know. We have heard all about those cell phones. Sit down and lets discuss something about your appearance."

Astonished, I exclaimed, "okay, now you are really scaring me!"

"I see the first thing you did was to rub your face;" she said.

"I know that I need a shave and a haircut, but that never entered my mind until now."

"That's it exactly." Jan said. "I have 2 kinds of lotion with me. One controls hair growth. I will cut your hair to your liking and then rub this lotion in. The lotion will prevent new hair growth. You can use it for ear and nose hairs also. The other lotion is for your face. I see that you like to be clean shaven, no mustache or beard. I will put this lotion on your face carefully as not to get it into your hair. You will leave this lotion on until we go to the showers when we get to the farming area. Once you go through the shower, you will never need a haircut or ever have to shave again."

Jan and I went out back. There was a parking lot with a few vehicles. She led me to one and told me it was mine. She handed me a disc and showed me where to put it. A small compartment contained another disc.

Each disc will last 1 year, so when vehicle stops, just change the disc. Another will be made to put in the compartment. Jan told me to drive and get used to my new transportation device.

A young woman approached us as we were preparing to leave and said hello. Jan handed her a list of food and pills that I had made out earlier. She thanked us and went on her way.

We headed for the farming area. Jan explained that it was harvesting time here and many from other sections were here to help. We visited for a short time and then headed for the other section where the animals were. I saw horses, cows, pigs, sheep and chickens. Jan told me the horses are not used in the making of the food. Jan began to explain. When one cow dies, the doctors will take parts of the cow and other parts will go to the factories. One cow can give them the taste of meat and milk for a year for everyone on the Island. No one eats the actual meat or drinks the milk. The remainder of the cow is taken to the end of the section to be buried.

The showers were our next stop before heading to one of the factories. We went to the main street and Jan showed me where to park. We entered one of the larger buildings on the street. The first room wasn't very big. There were 2 aisles from one side to the other. There was a shelf on each side of the aisles and each shelf was divided into sections. Each shelf contained about 250 bins. All of the bins were filled with crackers and labeled with numbers. Plastic bags were at each bin.

"You can come here at anytime and help yourself," Jan said. "It's just like going to a supermarket. A book like the one you have is by the door. If you left something off your list, you may pick it up on our way out. Let's go into the next room."

The next room was even smaller. There was only one aisle and the bins on the shelf were filled with different sizes and shapes of crackers. "This is where you get the food for your pets," Jan said.

The next room is the main room where we manufacture our food. There are 8 factories on the main street that we will visit. We continued on and met some of the factory workers. One of the workers showed me around and explained the operations of this factory. We stopped by a large bowl. The factory contained 10 bowls. Each bowl is filled with the ingredients to make the crackers, water is added and mixed thoroughly. The flavor was then added and let set for about 15 minutes and then mixed again. The mixture is then poured on a tray. The tray goes on a conveyor where the crackers are formed and shaped. The crackers are then taken to the bins that I saw upon entering the building.

"This looks so easy!" I exclaimed. "A food processing plant with no ovens, freezers or packaging material."

Jan said it was easy and added, "And once again all are working together. Even the scientist who make the flavoring trade jobs frequently to help out. All of our factory workers are able to perform each job. When we finish our tour of the entire Island, you may come back here to work with the people.

Before we leave, I'd like to make a suggestion. I know how much you love pizza and we have copied the flavor of the Misty Mountain pizza, but only the sauce and dough recipe is used for the crackers. To add other ingredients, you may pick up other flavorings like pepperoni, hamburger, sausage or anything else you like with your pizza. Just take a bite of each cracker and chew them together. I see you are already making a list, so we'll pick up some things and head back to your house."

We passed another small room on the way out that had bins of the pills.

We arrived at my blue house and entered an unlocked door. I found everything I'd ordered earlier on the table, along with a little white pill. Jan reminded me of the extreme importance of taking the white pill every night. She also expressed how much she wanted me to remain on the Island. I usually shower twice a day and feel we should go there now. When we shower and relax in the pond, we will come back here and sit in the yard for awhile before we go to the entertainment building.

"I will not forget to take the pill!" I am curious about so many things and need to find the answer of why I was brought here."

We finished our showers, went back to my house and had some snacks. There were people getting off work who joined us and took turns asking me questions about my life in Misty Mountain. When travelers returned to the Island, everyone would gather to learn about their journeys. The people here were very well informed about what was going on in the world. There were so many little things they did not know about and I knew I could be of help later on.

A lady known as Ruth joined us. She was holding a puppy. "This is for you."

Astonished, I muttered a thank you to Ruth. I added that puppies are the most beautiful animals in the world. I held him up and fell in love. He was black with a little white spot on his head. "I'm going to call you Star."

"Good name." Jan said. "I knew of your dog Star back home. That must have been a very sad moment for you."

"Yes, it was, but then I got Misty. I know I have only been here 3 days, but not a moment goes by without thinking of my friends of Misty Mountain and Misty. This little guy is going to be a huge comfort to me."

Jan was reminding me that it was time to go to the entertainment building. She told me to leave Star in the yard and neighbors would watch him and he would be inside when we return.

We walked a short distance to the entertainment building. I walked in and was overwhelmed at the size. Tables and chairs filled the room and there was probably over 1,000 people there, yet, the room seemed only half full. From the center of the room, someone stood up to motion us to come over. We made our way to the center and found 5 tables saved for us. My 4 friends were already there. At one side of the room was a very long bar. Jan told us to help ourselves to food and drink there. I went over and picked up some pizza and beer. Two other people had joined Jan at our table when I returned.

Jan introduced Jack. "Jack is one of the scientists who works with land and farming. This is Sophia who is also a scientist and works at the ocean."

Most of their conversation was about their work and the animals. Whenever someone made a new discovery, everyone in the room would quiet down and listen to the new developments.

The people are always excited to hear reports and stories from returning travelers. Everyone gathers to listen to what the happenings of the world are. You and the other 4 who were brought here can be a great help by informing us of all the little things going on in your countries, both good and bad.

"I'll do the best I can." I replied. "I know you have read my magazines and I really only want to talk about good things, but there is so much evil and dis-respect in the world today. I don't even want to get started because I may not be able to stop. I want to listen to your travelers and help fill in details. I believe they will like what I have to say and I will try to keep things as simple as possible."

Jan reminded me that no pressure would be used and said to feel free to speak at any time to anyone about anything. There is one more thing I want to talk about and that is sex. "We are all human and have sexual desires. Now, come with me."

We followed Jan to the end of the room that had a wide opening that led to another room. A lot of people were here in this large room. "Everyone in this room will have sex tonight" Jan said. "As soon as they choose a partner, they leave and go to one of their homes to have sex. This room empties quickly. Towards the end of the evening, and some have not found a partner, someone from the other room will volunteer to be a partner so everyone will have sex. There are some couples who do stay together for a few weeks, but if one wants to have sex and the other does not, they come here and have sex with someone else. It's been this way forever and there have never been problems.

"Wow! What a way to cure ones sexual desires." I said. "This would never happen in the world. This is something I really need to know more about."

I could hear the evening music and told Jan I would like to go home now and think about my day. During the walk home, Jan wanted to mention something else about sex. "You will never have sex with someone other than their race. We are all born here within our own race. We have no mothers or fathers because we are all family. All those born here have the love and respect from everyone, not only from their own race, but from everyone. We are one very big happy family."

I asked if Jan would sit and discuss the sex in more detail when we got to my house. I will try to keep it short and simple the way things are done at home. She agreed.

My new little friend met me. I got us some beer and pizza and we sat down.

"I really don't quite know where or how to begin." I began. " I have not heard religion or God mentioned here. Religion is very important at home or it used to be. Sometimes I wonder how many Gods there are. I remember when I was attending school, one of my friends dated this girl. They were both white and in love, but could not marry because he was Catholic and she was a Baptist. Some things have changed in past 50 years though. Today, couples are married raising families from different religions and even different races. I don't know if the churches accept this or not. So many of our youth are dating outside their race. Inter-racial sex is even being promoted through TV and movies. Just one time, I'd like to hear a white woman say to a black man trying to pick her up that she does not believe in inter-racial relationships, but they could be friends. I could go on and on about this subject. Maybe I'm not the person that should be here and you may want to send me back. I really do want to stay and learn more, especially why I was brought here."

"I really hope the things you learn from us do not discourage you in any way. If what you say about religion is true, then you will not find religion here. You can say we are one huge happy family that love and care for each other and evil does not exist!"

"Jan, I want you to know that in just 3 days here, I have witnessed more respect than I've seen in my entire life."

Jan said it was late and time for her to go. She said good-night and would see me in the morning. I went in with my new little friend, took my pill and fell asleep.

The next few days consisted of visiting all the factories on the street. I was amazed at how things were made and how easy it was to accomplish.

The building that fascinated me the most was the Library. I wasn't that big and there were not the volume of books I expected. Jan explained that every book is written in English, except for the dictionaries. The English version was not as large as the ones I have at home. All the words were simple ones that everyone understands. Communication is of utmost importance here and must be kept simple and easy to understand in all languages. That sounded great to me. This would be great back home.

Many things started to flood my mind, the books the schools and colleges use, government papers, the different contracts insurance and doctors use and know that less than half the people at home understand the contracts. And how about the so-called smart people using words that no one knows to start up a conversation. To me, the smart people are stupid because they can't communicate with everyone. Jan then showed me hundreds of other dictionaries containing languages of the world. All words were same and this will be helpful when I learn to speak the other languages.

On my 5th day, I went to meet my neighbor. Jan introduced me to John. Jan left us and informed John she was anxious to hear his report.

I asked John if we had met before. He smiled and told me we have never really met. "I am one of the travelers here and whenever I travel to the United States, I go to Misty Mountain. I have made several trips there and always go to Tom's bar. I keep a low profile and am there to just listen. I guess you could say that I'm the one responsible for you being here. I'll explain all about that at a later time. So, what do you think of our Island?"

"I'm still very confused." I confessed. "I feel this is a dream and I don't want to wake up. At the end of every day, I have many questions and are always answered by being told that I would learn about that later. I do have one question for you and I think I know what the answer will be but have to ask anyway. Are you the one responsible for the mist at Misty Mountain?"

John laughed. "In a way, yes I'm responsible, but not just me alone, but everyone here. You are correct and you will learn all about the mist a little later."

I laughed back. "You are so lucky I have a lot of patience. Most everyone I know would be going out of their minds by now and demanding answers."

"I know how hard this is on you. When you meet with Joseph in 6 months, all of your questions will be answered. You have a few more days with your orientation with Jan and then will be free to do whatever you like. I would like to go with you a few times;"

"I would like that. How many trips do you make to the United States? Would you mind checking on my friends, especially Lorrie?" I asked.

"I'll do that." John said. "I don't think you have to worry about Lorrie. She is very special and your disappearance will remain a secret with her. I can't interfere with anyone or anything while on my journeys. I will tell you everything about your friends and especially their work."

We sat outside all night. Several stopped by to welcome John back. John's dog was returned by a neighbor who was looking after him during his absence. Star took to him right away. It was fun to watch the dogs playing. The music was half over and both dogs laid down. The affect the music has on animals just amazes me. It was time to go home and get to bed.

I woke early the next morning and went outside to wait on Jan. We went to visit the school and hospital areas today which are beside each other. The school was not large and only children attend school are from ages 3 thru 10 years old. The teachers do not do all the teaching. The older children help considerably. The teachers taught about the Island. The children chose their particular interests. They were instructed in their interests. When they reached age 10, they would go to work in their areas of interest. I don't know how, but things always seemed to work out. Most had a particular interest and at least one would be interested in the field of scientific discovery. Sometimes a child would show no interest in anything and they would be sent to the animal hospitals to care for the sick animals. The animals were all very intelligent and showed love and respect for the children and never left them alone. The kids learned to love and respect all the animals. They fed the animals and took an interest when the animal became sick and ask doctors many questions. The doctors instructed the kids how to care for the sick animals. We knew them as vets back home.

I kept questioning myself on just where does all this intelligence come from. I was told that babies born here are born with 30 per cent use of their brains. And, once again I was told I would know more about this when I met with Joseph.

The next few days were spent touring all sections and visiting with the people. The best part was getting to see all the animals and the section of Africa was my favorite. I got to be part of feeding all the animals and loved being there with the elephants and chimpanzees.

When we entered the different sections, people would only speak English while I was there. The different sections had their own languages and everyone knowing all the languages made it easy. It was all about respect.

Now I understand that uncomfortable feeling when I visited a foreign country. I know I will have to learn to speak many languages while I'm here. People speak in their own language, even when everyone around them only speak English. No one ever knew what they were saying and we always wondered if they were talking about us, but guess we'll never know. It's all about respect.

The last 3 days with Jan turned out to be the most interesting. The first was spent at the ocean. Sophia joined us and was very helpful in explaining the things they do. The only thing I knew about ocean life was from TV or books. People on this planet have no idea of what the ocean has to offer. I knew I would be spending a lot of time here. Sophia and Jan took me to a large building located near the ocean and Sophia mentioned there was another one like this on the other side of the Island. We entered and I saw only 5 people working here. After the introductions, Sophia explained the operation. They possess a lot of these little machines that travel to every part of the ocean and collect plant life and then it's analyzed. There were thousands of specimens present. We entered another room where engineers were constructing the machines. The crafts measured only about 3 foot in length and about a foot and a half wide. One of the engineers showed me how it was constructed. Each one has 3 compartments where specimens were stored to be brought back to the Island. All of this was controlled by computers in the other room. All the crafts were installed with a radar jamming device that made it impossible for any detection. Sophie showed me how this was accomplished. She sat at the computer and programmed the craft that had collected its last specimen to return to the Island. She showed me that she was raising the craft near the surface where she would set the craft at maximum speed of around 100 mph. They use this speed when they are near the surface, around 20 foot under water. As they approach the destination, the craft is slowed down and submerges very slowly so it won't bother or harm any of the ocean creatures.

We left the building to go outside to sit and talk. Sophia continued to tell me they only have about 5,000 crafts and need about that many more. The oceans are so vast and so full of beautiful life. People of the planet are just beginning to know its true beauty, but then again, there are those with absolutely no respect for the ocean and its habitants. The military and governments are exploding bombs and submarines caring nuclear weapons are destroying ocean life and for what reasons? The answer to that is power and greed. They are killing our whales for money and greed. As we began to leave, Sophia promised me that the killing of the whales would soon come to an end.

I knew I would be returning to the ocean again soon.

My days ended with Jan and I was lost my first day all alone. I just didn't know where to start. Star and I would take long walks and visit with the residents. I started my days at the library for a couple hours and at the end of every day, I would go to different sections to watch the animals and observe their reactions to the nightly music. The music had the same affect on all of them. After a couple weeks, I couldn't believe that I was learning, not only words but complete sentences in many of the different languages.

A few weeks passed and I find that I'm spending most of my time alone. I would sit with Star and just think of my friends at home and wish I could be there with them or have them here with me. I started going to one side of the Island and sit alone with Star. One afternoon, I noticed a baby seal about 100 yards away. Star ran over and wanted to play with the seal. The little seal was not frightened at all. They became very good friends during the next few days. The seal even approached me and the three of us had some very good times.

Time was going by fast. I spent more time with Ivan, Luis, Kwan and Sarah. We still had no idea of why we were brought here.

I woke one morning and Jan was outside waiting for me. She informed me 6 months have passed and it is time for me to see Joseph.

Chapter VI

Luis, Ivan, Kwan, Sarah and I were sitting together at a table. The room was very familiar, as it was the same room I sat in when I first arrived here. There were quite a few people sitting and talking. Joseph and 4 other people were sitting at a large table at the front of the room. I learned the other 4 were mentors of my friends. Jan was sitting at another table with the other 4 guides. Another 15 people occupied another large table. John, my neighbor was the only one I recognized and learned the others were all travelers.

Joseph stood and smiled. "I'm so very glad to see that you have all decided to stay here with us. This does not surprise me at all. Our travelers did an excellent job with their first 5 selections. I know you have learned a lot and I will continue this in English and do believe you can all understand me. For the next 6 months you will begin to know some of our secrets. The first thing I want to talk about is the pill you take before you go to bed. I will call it brain food so you can try to understand the power of it. Many years ago, our scientists started sending the little crafts into the ocean to collect plants from the bottom. Not only did they do research on these plants, but plants from every part of the world. While experimenting with the plants, a great discovery was made. The pill was created with 1,147 ingredients. The ocean plants provide 971 and the other 276 ingredients come from plants of other countries. Everything in this pill is sent directly to the brain, every brain cell is nourished. This explains how you have learned so much in such a short time.

Then they wanted to hear our thoughts and reactions to what we have learned over the last 6 months. We all talked in turn and spoke for hours. We all had similar feelings that this was a bit strange, the bathroom the showers, etc. We agreed the hardest thing to get used to was the food and missed our food from home. But we all admitted that we have never felt better or healthier in our life.

They asked us about our lives back home, both good and bad. I enjoyed hearing about my friends. I realized there weren't just problems in my country, but more problems existed all over the world that I was unaware of. I spoke mostly about my friends and the love that family members have for each other. I added the respect I have for my friends. I told of many good people who have respect of this planet and have a love for the animals. I kept bad thoughts to myself and made it short. It was all about the lack of respect that humans have for each other and all things on the planet. One major concern that we all shared was the over-population and it's only getting worse. The beauty of this planet is slowly being destroyed.

"I would like to thank you for your opinions. It's going to be up to you very special 5 people to start making a difference in the world. The remaining 6months will be spent working with our travelers. There is a room in this building called our computer room. Our computer system will provide you with the knowledge of changes that can be made right away to benefit the people of this planet and that can only be accomplished by you 5 people. We will teach you and provide help but we can not interfere with what has to be done. We have discussed this among ourselves and we have all agreed that what we do will not affect our beliefs and at no time will we take any physical actions to change the world. We can only advise. If at any time during the next 6 months you disagree with anything we are doing and would like to return home, that would not be a problem. We will send you home and you will not remember anything about your stay with us." Joseph continued, "But, with your help, we figure it will take about 100 years before people can learn to live together in peace and it will be done. You , Bob, have already made a difference with the work you did at Misty Mountain. Through your work, people are learning all about respect. They are slowing down and thinking about their decisions. We will take a little break now and go get some fresh air. We will go to the computer room when you return.

We went outside and were left alone to talk. My 4 friends and I still didn't have a clue as to why we were brought here. We did not want to return home. We went back inside and were escorted to the computer room.

There were at least 150 computers throughout the room. Joseph informed us that we would be spending a great deal of our time here in the next few months. Joseph continued, "there is so much that we have to teach you and we will be patient and try not to rush you. This will not consume all of your time and you will still have time to go and do the things you want to do. Each of the computers have a function. We are aware of how much your computers at home store, but you will see how much more advanced our system is. When travelers return from their trips, they put the information gathered into the appropriate computer. I'm going to be leaving now and will return in about 6 months. Your time will be spent with our travelers and they will be your teachers.

The travelers gave us a quick tour and then we split up. John and I went home and we sat outside his house. "You have been here 6 months Bob and haven't even seen a computer before today. You can see just how life is without computers and its seems simple. I know that back home in your country, computers are very important and people depend on them for everything. Almost everything is computerized now and it's only going to get worse."

"You are so right, John. In this day and age the computers seem to control everything. They make things run more efficiently and the people do depend on them a lot. It's amazing how much information can be stored. Our children and teachers use the computers a lot, but I still prefer books. One thing I never liked about the computer world is the video games. The kids and adults have become addicted and become lazy. Another invention I'm not fond of is the cell phones. I would guess that only 5 per cent of all cell phone calls are emergencies or business. People just love to talk and can't seem to go 10 minutes without looking at information or talking to someone on their cell phones."

John laughed. "I know all about the cell phones, but you will be using them a lot when you go back home. There will be many important people you must speak with."

John and I sat in his yard and he prepared me for the next day. I played with Star and listened to the music. I went home, had another beer before going to sleep.

I had a lot of things going through my head as John and I walked to the main building. I didn't say anything. We reached the main building and went directly to the computer room.

"The intelligence you have gained in past months will make things I'm going to show you easier to understand. You would of thought of this as impossible 6 months ago. Let's sit down at this computer and we will begin. This computer has a little over 1,000 names of people who we will eventually bring here to the Island to teach the same things we are teaching you now. You will find all their personal information, such as addresses and what they do for a living. In the future, more names will be added to this list. We will start bringing 10 people at a time and some will probably not stay and will be sent back home. We will not start doing this until your year is up and then proceed to bring 10 every 3 months. All of these people have seen the mist in their own country and they still believe, as you did, that there is something good about it. There have been others witness the mist but have forgotten or just did not care, but the ones we are concerned with are the ones who still believe and care. Our travelers have followed and collected information on them for years and is stored here in the computer.

The rest of the day, John took me to every computer in the room except one. To obtain information seemed very simple, not because of my added education of computers, but it seemed at least 20 steps have been eliminated. It was very nerve racking at home and they say it's easy. It's only easy if you have a knowledge of computers.

Later I met with my 4 friends to discuss our day. We talked about the past 6 months and found a lot to laugh and joke about. Kwan informed us that she had sex with a couple of men. We decided to go to the entertainment building and have a couple beers. I found out that I was the only one who has not had sex yet. I've been so caught up in everything sex had not even crossed my mind, until now. After a couple beers and some pizza, I went home with Sophia and spent the night. I told her in the morning that I was very attracted to her and she reminded me that all we did was to relieve ourselves of sexual desires. She reminded me about how sex is on the Island and no jealousy when we decide to spend the night with someone else. She talked a little more about sex and said all the right things to make me understand. As I walked to the shower, I realized that I'm really going to enjoy myself these next few months.

I spent the next 2 weeks in the computer room. Every day, I would leave amazed at what I had learned. After 2 weeks, I spent only half days with the computers and spent the rest of my time visiting the other sections and helping feed the animals. I spent time taking Star to the ocean to play with the little seal. It was so much fun watching them.

I started to have sex frequently, but found myself spending a lot of my time alone again. I spent time with Star, relaxing and listening to the music and doing a lot of thinking of Lorrie, Brittany, Mark and Misty back home. I just couldn't wait until I could see them again.

Time was passing quickly and the year was drawing to an end. I had learned every computer except 1 and knew that was a special one. The next 2 weeks, I spent alone. The night before my meeting with Joseph, I spent the night with Jan. We walked to the main building the next morning.

"We have been anxiously waiting for this day to come," Joseph said with a smile. "You will spend the next 2 days here with me. I will show you everything stored on our main computer. From the information you receive will contain your assignments of what we would like you to do. We know of all the problems on earth and all the good things also. Our people on the Island can not interfere or change the things on earth. We cannot change the way people act or what they do. We can help you make changes that will save the planet. Some of these changes will probably take over 100 years and we won't be around to see the results. You 5 people will be responsible for getting things started. We have it all set up for you and everything that you will be responsible for will not attract attention to any of you. Everything we start will be for the good of all humans in the future. People in high places will make trouble and there will be a lot of chaos all over the world. People will be blaming others for the things happening. Just remember one thing, the result will always be good. People will begin to learn and adjust. Until then, things will be confusing and a lot of bad things will happen. There will be a list of things on a disc we will give you. You will need to work together on this and if you need advice, our travelers will be available. After we take a break, please put your disc into one of our computers and study it closely. We will return in a couple of hours.

After we viewed our discs, we just could not believe what we saw. We sat speechless and stared at each other. When the others entered the room, we had a lot of questions, but we stopped when Joseph stood to explain.

"I hope that nothing you have seen on the disc upsets or frightens you in any way."

Joseph continued, "We know that the world is in bad shape and it's only going to get worse. With all the information our travelers have gathered over many years convinced us to come to a decision that something must be done. Since we cannot interfere, we decided to bring people from your world here and teach you how to make the world a better place. This is a beautiful planet with many secrets. Our scientists are very busy uncovering these secrets and finding solutions to the existing problems of today. Most of the things on the disc will not be used by you right away, and the people that follow you will have the task of solving most of the problems. We asked for your opinions on problems in your countries. Our travelers gave the same responses we received from you. For now, it seems that oil is a large part of survival of all humans. Oil is the topic of many conversations today and the cost has skyrocketed. All transportation depends on oil. You have seen our transportation here and not one drop of oil is needed. This planet needs oil and when it's gone the planet will die. Our scientists have the knowledge to construct automobiles, airplanes trucks and all vehicles that currently use oil into ones that do not require oil. The ones following you will see that these vehicles are manufactured. In another disc, there are names of people to contact in your country. Some of these people are very close to finding the solution but are many years away. These are the ones that will be contacted and will start manufacturing vehicles immediately. They will be better, cheaper to build and will sell for less money. In a few years, there will not be the automobile industry as you know it today.

"Next, we will discuss the business world. Everything on the planet will be improved and made at a cheaper cost. The public will pay less for a better product. Another disc contains names of very intelligent people without a college degree because of lack of money. They have been working hard to make a living. These are the people who will be contacted to run our businesses. There will be no bosses and everyone will do their equal share of work. All profits will be divided equally. We figure 95% will be long term employees.

Our next topic is the farming industry around the world. Nature plays a big role and we can't do anything about that. Our scientists have developed a way of turning ocean water into fresh water that will enable farmers to grow crops where they never could before. Our irrigation systems will make it possible to get fresh water to any part of the planet.

These are just a few things we are going to change and everything I have just spoken of will take lots of money.

Money is the most important part of your mission. You know how much money there is in the world and who has most of it. There is dirty money and greed. This is what we are going to do, and please excuse me for using this word, we are going to steal it! These people will not be able to survive without their money. This is the first job you will do. It won't take long and we will have more than enough to complete our mission. Step 1 on your disc is drug money. We have a list of every drug dealer on the planet, their phone numbers and bank account numbers. The list contains every dealer from the top to the street dealers who sell to school children. All this money will disappear. With our computers, we can intercept and transfer funds and will take every penny. This is going to start war among the drug people who will be blaming each other. This will also make a big impact on the government agencies who profit from drugs. These Politician's and government officials will see their money disappear also. The drug dealers will start dealing on a cash only basis but most will be killed for the money.

The rich people who cheat on taxes will also see their money disappear. When we start our businesses, the government will want to raise our taxes. That is not a problem with us, because we do everything legal and obey all laws and we will pay taxes with their own money. Our travelers will be there to guide and help you. No one will suspect you and our computer system will protect you. There is no possible way to break in to our system. We can always detect when someone gets close. It only takes seconds to change our codes and numbers.

You 5 people will work together and help each other out as much as possible. We will continue to steal money from bad people. For example, Sarah, you have your own dirty money to steal. I think you will enjoy this part. In the disc, you will discover the names of every poacher on the planet, who they work for and their locations when they think it is safe to hunt the elephants. Within a year, there will not be 1 elephant killed for ivory. The same will go for the whalers. Many Swiss bank accounts will disappear.

When you arrive back home, you will continue to live the life that you did before you were brought here. You will all do a lot of traveling the first few months and will be accompanied by our travelers. You will go to many parts of the world. The travelers will not be going through any custom check points because they will be carrying large amounts of pills. They will give the pills to you and you will drop 5 pills into every lake, river and reservoir or wherever you find fresh water. You all agreed the over-population was a major problem and the pills will solve this in time. They are harmless. They contain a chemical that allows women to only give birth one time. It will take many years before the public realizes women can only have one child. It will be hard on the kids growing up. We try to teach them about safe sex but doesn't seem to work. Maybe they will learn to think long and hard before they have sex. We are going to leave you alone again for a couple hours so you may discuss what we have given you today.

We did a lot of talking during those 2 hours. I listened most of the time and we laughed a lot. We were thinking about the fun we could have with this. Everyone was very excited, but I had different thoughts. Just before

Joseph and the others returned, I stood up to make a toast. "You know that in a few days, we will be the smartest people on earth, except the people here on the Island. To think that 5 people from 5 different countries could come to love and respect each other, maybe these people know what they are doing. This could be the start of a very good thing!"

Joseph and the others walked in as we finished our toast. "Do you have any questions to ask us at this time?"

Ivan was the first to speak. "Many of our questions have been answered except for a couple. Why us? We don't know why we are here."

"I can answer that question now." Joseph went on to explain. "It all has to do with the mist. I will start at the beginning. We needed a way to get some people here to teach them our ways. Our travelers spent a lot of time looking for a solution. They found 9 locations where the atmosphere and environment were perfect. These 9 locations were just right for us to make the mist appear and disappear. As you know, through Bob's work, that each are located in mountains, have a small village near-by and there is a beautiful valley below a cliff. Our travelers placed 3 machines around the valley. The machines would not be found or detected by anyone. When the weather conditions are right, we turn on the machines that create the mist. They also installed the same kind of instruments that create the music you hear on the Island each night. The frequency is a lot lower and can't be heard by humans, only animals. The dogs could hear it and that is why they relaxed and were so peaceful. Bob's work through his magazine has sent a message to the entire world. People began to believe there was something good about the mist. You 5 people felt very strongly about the mist, and out of millions who have seen the mist, only about 5% still believe that there is something very good here. Others have forgotten or just don't care. The people who still believe in the mist will follow in your footsteps and be brought here like you were. Now you know about the mist and why you were brought here. There are many other things you will have to learn from our computer system and by the end of tomorrow, you will know exactly what it is we will need you to do. There will always be a traveler available to help you. I want to take this time to wish you all the best of luck and thank you for spending the entire year here with us. Good-bye and thank you again!"

Joseph and the travelers left the room. My 4 friends and I went outside to sit and visit. They did most of the talking, as I was in one of my quiet moods. I had a lot going through my mind. Thousands stopped by to wish us luck and say their good-byes. There was something very important on my mind that I needed to speak with Joseph about. I had a hard time going to sleep.

As John and I walked to the main building, I asked John, "before we get started today, could I speak to Joseph and the travelers alone without my 4 friends?"

"I can arrange that." John said. "Give us a little time to get the others started."

We gathered in the computer room and were given the 5 discs to look at. They then gave us the 6th disc and were informed that it was the most important. When the others busied themselves, John and the other travelers took me to see Joseph..

"I would like to thank you for taking time and listening to what I have to say, " I started. "When I first arrived here, I was confused and a little frightened and very curious. It was all so strange, but by watching and listening, every day became easier to deal with. Your way of life and especially your care, love and respect for the animals made me feel good. I am beginning to understand now. I now know why you want to keep your home here a secret and I respect your decision not to interfere with what is going on in the world today. The world is in bad shape, but it is a good world. It is understood that you can't do anything physically and that is why we are here. We are to become teachers without anyone knowing. People will have to adjust to survive. This will all take time and there will be some who will not be able to adjust to changes. The ones who work together and respect each other will adjust easily. Many greedy people with mass amounts of money will not survive. Those who stop and think about decisions will also survive. I am aware that I will not be around to see a beautiful world where people have learned to respect each other. There are a lot of things that I will not be able to explain when I return home and one thought came to mind, I have not had a shave or get hair cut for a whole year."

Joseph laughed. "One of the discs has the formula for that. A product with this formula will be available to the barbers. They have a respectable business and many will go out of business. A profit will be made by them on this product. The product will not be used on anyone under the age of 21 and the warnings will be printed very clearly and every barber will know what it is used for."

"That will be great." I said. "There are so many things that are going to happen, good things, and this may be selfish on my part, but I won't be around to see the results. I see a lot of chaos and people wanting to profit off everything. I would love to see how families react when they learn they can only bear one child. I can only vision a lot more love and respect and better communication in all families. Now, I will get to the point of why I wanted this conversation with you. Not one day passes that I do not think about my friends at home and seeing the differences in the way of life." I paused for a few minutes before continuing. "What I would like to know is there rules or laws that exist that prevent an outsider to live here? I would like to remain here on the Island and live the rest of my life."

Joseph looked at me and smiled. He didn't discuss anything with anyone. "Bob, we really didn't figure on this but we don't have any rules or laws. Yes, you may stay here with us and I know we can learn a lot from you. You could be very helpful working with the next group our travelers bring here. I believe your presence will make our new guests a little more relaxed and that will make things easier for us......So, welcome to our Island."

We went to join the others. Joseph quickly got every ones attention and made the announcement. I spent the rest of the day going over the discs with my friends. We covered most of it. Luis has been to the United States a few times and he would take care of the fresh water supply there. The others would work together stealing the drug money.

My friends and I had a toast at the end of the day and wished each other luck. I then went home to Star. I got a beer and sat with Star on my lap and tears fell, but they were good tears. I went to bed and fell fast asleep.

Chapter VII

I woke up the next morning with a different feeling about myself. For the first time in a long time, I didn't have much to think about as most all my questions had been answered. After breakfast, Star and I went outside to sit in the yard. John joined us and I knew he would be able to help me out with a few things on my mind.

"Good morning Bob" John cheerfully greeted me.

"Good morning John. I'm hoping you can help me out with a few things. Over the past year, I've become aware of everything going on here and want to know where my part in the community will be. I have to have something to do and want to do my equal share. I don't have a clue as to where to begin."

"Your decision to remain here came as a big surprise last night. We discussed this for hours after you left and did come up with a solution. I was to return to your home with you, but now I will stay here with you until the next person from your country has spent a year here and is ready to be sent back. I'm going to work with you and show you how we communicate with your 4 friends that are returning home. You will learn a lot from me and we will all benefit from your knowledge. Let's walk to the shower and we can talk on the way."

"I can't wait to hear this! Just what is there that I can possibly teach you?" I asked.

John laughed. "I have spent a lot of time in your country and have learned that sports are a very big part of peoples lives. I have brought some information home from my trips on sports. Our people were very interested at first and then when I informed them on the professional sports, all the fighting involved and the money issues, well, they became uninterested.

What we want from you is to teach us about sports, all about the fun and exercise and achievements you can get by competing. Can you do that?"

"I sure can People can have fun and get a lot of satisfaction, win or lose, from sporting events. In most sports, all you need is a ball and some other equipment. I really loved slo-pitch softball and was pretty good but because of traveling I missed a lot of games. You get friends together and form teams. Some teams were very good and winning was very important. Everyone has a position and performs to the best of their ability to achieve a win. One thing that bothered me was the show-off's that thought they were invincible and above the law. They would dress like gangsters, wear their hats funny, the only message I got from them was, 'Look at me! Look at me!' It was like a cry for attention from them. If only they would have played as good as they thought they were. There will be no show-offs here."

"There are a lot of things like this we want to learn from you." John said. "Another thing we would like for you to do is to spend time with the next 10 people we will be bringing here. We were aware that the first couple weeks, all of you had thoughts about not taking the pill a few times. We really don't expect everyone to stay the full year, but if you could offer encouragement, maybe they will stay. Out of the 10 coming, 2 will be Americans, but since you now know all the languages, you will spend time with all of them. We just ask you to be patient , go slow and let them make their own decisions."

"I know exactly what you mean. I can do all this and still find time to spend with Star and visit the computer room."

The next few weeks were spent with John in the computer room. He went over the discs and explained what they wanted to do. I was still amazed at how much information each disc contained. My friends had their discs when they returned home.

On 1 disc that everyone had and would work together on was the one containing the names and bank accounts we were going to steal the money from. John showed me the process and no one would ever be able to trace this money that will be deposited in accounts around the world.

John started on another disc. "I will give you an example of how we are going to open our own businesses. You will see how all the automobiles and other kinds of transportation will be built and sold. The construction will be better and the expense will be cheaper and none will ever need a drop of oil to run. There are hundreds of names here and these are the people that will be hired by the people we send back. It will be up to them to hire the employees. These people will be in charge of production and sales of the vehicles. The names we have here are all very intelligent in the auto industry. Some have a college degree but would not work as management because of suit and tie dress codes. Very few of these names are bosses or work in sales even though they possess the knowledge to do so. We feel we have collected the very best minds in the business and have learned a few things from your magazine. Every employee will be equal, no bosses and all will benefit from an idea and all participate in the decisions made in the company."

I learned from this disc that all automobile manufacturer and dealer will be out of business in 3 years. The planet will be able to keep its oil and survive. The list goes on and on and the future really looks good. The most impressive thing was how the drug money would disappear. I knew there would be violence and killing among them. John made it sound so simple and without anyone suspecting that we were doing this.

Most of my time was spent with John in the computer room It was so amazing how everything was planned. The water supply and the drug money was already going on.

He then showed me the plans for the next 10 people that will be arriving in another week.

This was like a dream come true for me. The next week was spent playing with Star and visiting the other sections to help feed the animals. If this is a dream, please don't ever let me wake up!

I just couldn't believe how fast the 3 months have went! While in the yard one evening, John came over and said he would be gone a couple days. He was going to the United States to pick up 2 Americans. I started to prepare myself to meet them after they had finished with their orientations with Jan.

The days passed quickly and I met the 2 Americans. A man named Larry and a woman named Brenda. I don't recall ever meeting them but they both knew who I was.

They had both been to Misty Mountain and remembered me from there. I answered their questions the best I could and encouraged them to be patient, stick it out and to take the pill every night. I assured them they would be glad they stayed the whole year here.

I visited the other sections and met the other 8 people brought here. They were from 8 different countries and 1 spoke English. They all knew who I was because of my work at Misty Mountain. I was told that I inspired them to believe in the mist. I informed them I would be there for them and encouraged them to let the people here on the Island teach them as they had taught me.

John went back to my country for a few days and returned with every kind of ball used in all the sports. He told me the engineers will build anything else we need.

The word spread fast throughout the Island about the sporting programs. I would be at the school. I found that was the best place to set up the fields and courts. Thousands showed up every day. They were all aware of the sports and the rules. The information was in the library and most didn't want to get involved with sports because of what they had read but this was going to be different. The builders started making the equipment I'd requested. Ground was cleared and the fields were put in place. There was a basketball court, a tennis court, golf course, soccer field and a bowling alley. John then surprised me with a Frisbee. I showed everyone how the dogs liked to play Frisbee. The dogs loved it. I was just amazed to see all this done in such a short time.

I explained the rules of the game we were going to play. I told them umpires and referees were used back home but, here we will use the honor system. The player knows if he has committed a violation , is safe or out. Play the game by the rules and you will have a lot of fun. Some people are born with a natural ability to play certain sports, others become good at practicing a lot. We should all play together and have fun. Some of you can run fast and others are good jumpers, but one very important quality that can make you a good player is eye and hand contact. This gives good coordination and makes good athletes.

The doctors here will put emphasis on exercise and stretching. You need to do this faithfully so you won't get hurt or will not hurt yourself as much.

I paused and then added that at not time should you let fun and sporting events interfere with work.

I stayed very busy helping the newcomers and working with John, but always found time to take Star to the ocean.

Another year has flown by. Every 3 months, 10 more people were brought here. Out of the first 10, 2 decided not to stay and was told more would have went back home if it wasn't for my encouragement. Out of the next 40, 3 followed in my footsteps and decided to stay.

I began spending more time at the ocean with Lorrie, the name I gave the seal, and Star. This time was so precious to me.

John and the other travelers were gone and it was time for the next 2 people to return home and carry on their missions. I had a lot of time to think.

When John finally returned home, I asked him if I could have a meeting with him and Joseph. John asked if tomorrow morning would be alright.

We went to meet with Joseph. "Joseph, there has been something on my mind for quite some time and I need to ask you something." I started.

"Sure Bob, but first I'd like to thank you for what you have done for us here." Joseph said.

"Thank you, Joseph. I want to ask both of you if there is any chance of me returning to Misty Mountain for a few days to see my old friends. I know there will be no problem with me and the secret of the Island is safe with me." I pleaded.

"You know, Bob, I've been expecting this question from you for quite some time. We all knew and we wanted it to be your decision. The answer is yes! John can take you there and you can leave as soon as tomorrow if that's convenient for you." Joseph replied.

"Well Bob, that was easy." John said. "We can leave around 10 tomorrow."

I was so excited, I couldn't hardly speak. "I'll see you in the morning." I finally got the words to come out of my mouth.

John and I rode out to the ocean. "This is the first time I've been in your machine. It's very comfortable. Do I need to bring anything?" I asked.

"No, I have everything we need at my house in your country. For now, just sit back, relax and enjoy the trip. It will take about 20 hours." John replied.

When we started out, we were only about 20 feet under water and were going around 100 mph. "We will take our time on this trip, Bob, and will slow down a lot when we reach the bottom. There are many wonderful things I want you to see. If there are other vessels or submarines in the area, I slow way down. They can't detect us because of our capability to jam any radar device known to man so they won't even know we are here. I also slow way down when there is ocean life, as I will not harm anything living in the ocean. We will arrive on the west coast where my beach house is located near the Oregon and California boarder. It is the closest one to Misty Mountain . We have 4 other such houses, 2 on the east coast and 2 on the west coast.

We finally reached the coast and John stopped the craft and turned on some sort of device. He told me we would stay here for awhile until the coast is clear and won't be seen going ashore. We finally emerged and drove the craft up to a house and went into a garage. When we got out, John asked me to relax and stretch a bit. I watched him work on his craft. The work took about an hour as he took it apart and added some things to it to make it look like a jet ski.

"There," John said. "Now it won't cause suspicion. I always have to do this. Let's go inside and get ready for tomorrow. We won't be leaving until dark and we should arrive at Misty Mountain tomorrow morning. In case you're wondering, I do have some pills stored here. We will take only what we need. You will need some clothes to wear and I'm sure I have your size here."

We took our pill and went to bed. The beach house was very nice, a little isolated with only 2 other houses in sight. We napped and took off around 10 that evening. John had a nice sporting vehicle and lots of cash in the house. We took what we needed and left.

John told me a little of the happenings going on here and reminded me to watch what I say during my visit. We finally reached Misty Mountain and stopped at the motel just outside of town. It had turned out just as I had hoped. I was really getting excited as we drove into town. We parked at my old office and waited for the streets to empty. John let me out and said he was going to eat breakfast and would see me later at the bar.

I was standing on the porch of the office when I heard a familiar dog barking. I opened the door and Misty jumped in my arms. I just hugged my old friend and then came a scream from Brittany. She came running and just hugged and hugged me. Cheryl, Marks wife was the only other one in the office. I was being mugged by two of my best friends when Mark and Lorrie came running out of the back room to see what was going on. I shook Marks hand and Lorrie and I just looked at each other then hugged each other.

"Oh Bob, I thought I would never see you again, but deep inside, I always felt this day would come." Lorrie whispered in my ear.

With tears in my eyes, I whispered back to her. "Lorrie, I never did say good-bye and never will."

While we were all drying our eyes, Brittany was running around the room like she was lost. She was still just as funny as I remembered her.

"Brittany!" Mark yelled. "You know how to do this. It's called a toast!"

"Oh yeah!" Brittany said as she stumbled over to the refrigerator.

"A toast now would be perfect." I said. "But let's not say anything now and go to a place where a toast would be more appropriate and you all know where that is!"

"The office is officially closed." Mark shouted!

"I will give you guys 1 hour to be alone and then I'm coming to join you," Cheryl said.

We all laughed and Mark grabbed some beer and started off for the cliff. Mark carried the beer and I walked with my arms around Lorrie and Brittany. They held me so close I had trouble walking and breathing. Brittany did all the talking on the way. I looked into Lorrie's eyes and saw that puzzled look, but didn't say anything. We all sat down, had a few toasts and they were asking so many questions. I answered the best I could.

After a couple of hours, I told them I had been very busy and I'd met a new friend and you will all get to meet him at the bar a little later. I would like to be alone with Lorrie now and we will see you at the bar shortly.

Lorrie and I went over to the edge of the cliff and sat down. "I missed you so much," I said. "I can't explain what it was like the last time I saw you. There are so many things I would like to tell you, but I can't."

"I cried for days." Lorrie said. "Every night I said a prayer for you. I would think of Grandfather and in time the sadness went away. I knew in my heart that you were alright. I have so many questions and know you won't be able to answer them, but I 'm going to ask them anyway. None of the questions have to do with the way you left or the reason. I want to know if you know what is going on in the drug world. All of these people are killing each other and nobody knows why. There are so many articles about people in high places disappearing, I mean politicians and government people. Do you have anything to do with this?"

I smiled at her and shook my head no.

"But you do know who is responsible for this happening, don't you? She asked.

"Yes", I said smiling at her again. "But it really isn't what you think. Lorrie, please believe me. Think of your Grandfather and look deep into your mind and heart and think of the mist. There really is something good about it. I want you, Mark and Brittany to look at everything and you find only good to write about. I have read your work since I've been gone and the three of you are so talented about finding good things to write about. I have a little story about a small mid-western town. The things happening in this town were not good. Business people moved out, kids dropped out of school and left town. All of these people that left were connected in one way or another to drugs. Today, this small town is a better place to live, because it is a drug free environment and they are very happy. Inside this envelope are more stories to write about. Look deep into your heart and let your Grandfather be your guide."

"Oh Bob, I was so worried about you and now know I don't have to worry any more," Lorrie said as she put her arms around me and started to cry. "I am so very happy for you and believe me, no one will ever know your secret, whatever it is. I now know that you will always be with us. Don't worry about the stories, I learned from the best! Let's go to the bar now. I am anxious to meet your friend, John, but first I have to stop at the Photo store. Will you join me?"

I had quite a surprise at the Photo store. Lorrie introduced me to my God son, Robert! I had tears in my eyes as I held this beautiful boy and was so proud!

We arrived at the bar and I shook hands with Tom. Everyone was there and we all sat at our usual table. I introduced everyone to my friend John.

Lorrie got up and gave John a big hug. "Thank you for taking care of Bob." She whispered in his ear. "Don't worry about me because I will always be doing my part in making people aware of all the good things life has to offer."

John and I walked Lorrie home from the bar and said good night!

The next day at the office was a very touching scene. There were more tears as John and I left. It was a very long ride back to John's house. He really enjoyed this trip and said he understood what Lorrie meant. It was even a much longer trip back to the Island.

I just couldn't thank John enough for this trip and what he's done for me. I asked to be alone for the next few days.

After resting from the trip, I took Star to the ocean. We stayed all day and right before the sun set, Star came to put his head in my lap and Lorrie, my little seal came to lay her head in my lap also. We sat and watched the sun set just as the music started.

Chapter V111

After some alone time thinking about the time I spent with my friends and doing a lot of thinking. There were some things that troubled me. I could see the looks on their faces. Mark and Brittany seemed relieved about my whereabouts, but the look in Lorrie's eyes that she was not convinced and that she knew more, but would not talk about it. I felt so bad, not being able to tell them the truth. I decided to ask Joseph for help. Joseph had been spending every morning in the computer building now that the visitors had been sent back home and new visitors being sent home every three months.

The next morning I went over to the computer building and was glad to see John with Joseph.

"Hi Bob," Joseph said. "We have been waiting for you. Come sit with us and tell us about your trip. John has informed me that you handled yourself very well."

Bob paused a few seconds before speaking. "First of all, I would like to thank you for allowing me to see my friends. That meant a great deal to me, but there are some things that are really bothering me. I felt like I was lying to them but I never lied about anything. It was that I could not tell them the truth and understood that the truth could never be revealed. It was easy with Mark and Brittany because they were just so happy to see me but Lorrie had a shocked look at first but she kept it to herself. I spoke with her before I left and she told me that any secret I have would always be safe with her."

Bob looked down and then John had something to say. "Bob, we know that our secret will always be a secret. I wish there was something we could do."

"As a matter of fact, there is. I've given this a lot of thought and if you will hear me out, I have come up with a possible solution." Bob paused and continued. "What I would like to do is to have my pictures taken with all the different animals here in their native environments. The most important thing I have to ask you is if I could return to Misty Mountain every Christmas to spend with my friends. I would show the pictures and let the pictures speak. It would look as if I've been traveling to a lot of countries.

Joseph smiled at me. "Yes, that is one great idea and you may return every Christmas. John will be spending most of his time in your country, now that every three months new people will be brought here.

"Thank you very very much! You will never know how much this means to me." Bob replied.

"Joseph and I and others have been waiting for all this to happen. We have prepared for this day and now Joseph wants to speak with you." John said.

Joseph started, "I've been waiting for just the right time for this talk and I believe this is the time. I want to go into a little more detail about why you were brought here and to clarify some things you have learned about our Island. We have searched hundreds of years to find someone to bring here and teach him the way people live here. More important is the part they will play to help the people change to make the world a better place to live. It was your first issue of your magazine about the "mist" that brought you to our attention. Your belief in the "mist" allowed us to bring people together from around the world and to show you locations of the other eight mists. We followed your work as well as montering the work of Mark, Brittany and Lorrie. We knew you were the person we were looking for. We started to prepare the process of bringing you here. We had also told you that Lorrie was on our list also, but we decided she will be more valuable where she is by continuing writing her stories. Bob, you know the secret of Misty Mountain, the mist, the music, but no one knows yet that Lorrie is the real secret of Misty Mountain."

Bob spent the next few months in the computer building. Joseph would explain in more detail about what was being done about the money disappearing from people who dealt in illegal drugs. The public did not know anything about this because of the powerful people involved and certain secret government individuals. The suppliers and money started to disappear. The gangs with thousands of members started to blame each other which led to wars among themselves.

Joseph showed me a copy of the latest Dis-Respect magazine that my friends had just published. It was about the police involvement and neighborhood watches that dealt with gangs in neighborhoods all over the country. People and their businesses were constantly being terrorized by the street gangs and the police would do very little about it.

I read on and saw that the dis-respect was towards the politicians and law makers. So many of peoples rights are being taken away. One right that has not changed and that one is the right to bear arms. Everyone involved in crime of any kind uses this right.

After discussing things like this with Joseph, I mentioned that it would be nice to take away all the money from the people who make ammunition for these guns. What a funny sight to see all these criminals walking around with their guns and no bullets.

I showed Joseph a newspaper article about a young man who worked late night shift at a convenience store. Three men entered the store all armed with guns. The employee pulled his gun and shot all three. He was arrested and taken to jail. His attorney got him off with self-defense. A statement made in court by the attorney was one that all should remember 9-11 and that the President of the United States declared war on terrorism and this man was being terrorized.

The real hope I have is that for every story like this, there are thousands of other good stories about good and honest people found in the Respect magazines. We should not allow a handful of misguided individuals to ruin things. I wonder what our great ancestors like the authors of The Declaration of Independence and The Constitution of the United States would think of our world today. Would they want to tear it up and start over?

I left the computer building and took Star to the ocean to play with Lorrie. I just sat and thought about the last 60 years and all the changes and adapting to things. We all make adjustments as we grow. Sisty years ago, World War 11 was ending and many inventions and discoveries have been made. I looked back 120 years to the wild west, no automobiles or oil and there has always been violence of some type. I'm trying to picture 60 years from today and can't even imagine the future. There will still be violence around the world even with the help of my new friends. There are the children who refuse to listen to their parents and learn their life lessons in the streets and friends they hang out with. The respect must be taught early and enforced by parents. I don't see this happening in my lifetime, but I know it will eventually happen. As Star and I left the ocean, I wondered if there would even be anyone alive on this planet in 60 years and as quickly this thought came, I dismissed it from my thoughts.

The next few months went by quickly and I kept busy visiting and learning about new discoveries, working in the fields, attending the schools and playing games that I had taught and going to the entertainment center to listen to people talk about their day. My days usually would end sitting in the yard with Star and listening to the evening music.

While coming home one night, John yelled from his yard, "Bob, grab a beer and join me. I need to talk with you."

"Sure, I'll be right over. Is it Christmas time already?" I asked.

"Yes, it is. We will be leaving in a few days and I need to talk to you about our trip.

You will be doing the driving and I will be the passenger and I will monitor you. I want to make sure you know how to control the vessel because you will be making the return trip to the Island alone."

We sat and had a couple of beers and enjoyed the evening music and John went over more details of the trip. He told me it was very important that I take along enough pills.

Feeling a little nervous, we departed for the United States. I soon became confident and relaxed. The vessel seemed to run on its own with the computerized system. John suggested that I slow down on the way home and enjoy the beautiful ocean.

We reached the Oregon coast and John showed me more about the radar system. We did not want to be detected while moving the vessel to the garage for the dismantling process. All went well and we took a long nap before our trip to Misty Mountain.

We arrived at Misty Mountain early Friday and John told me to drop him off at the motel where he had a vehicle. He wished me luck and we said farewell.

It was too early to go to the office so I went to the restaurant. Mike was there and we had a nice visit and said the daily routines had not changed and everyone would be arriving soon. I was sipping my coffee when I heard a familiar scream. I turned to see Brittany running towards me. She jumped into my arms and starting asking questions.

Tom and Barb followed Brittany in and Tom came over to shake my hand. "As soon as I get my sister under control, I'd like to welcome you back."

"It's good to see you too and I will give you and Barb a good hug as soon as I'm released from Brittany." I laughed. It felt good to be in a room filled with happy people and lots of laughter.

Mark and Cheryl arrived and we exchanged hugs. The next familiar sound I encounter was Misty who jumped all over me and wouldn't quit licking me. Then Lorrie's voice,

"Okay, what did Brittany do now?"

I got up and went over to Lorrie and gave a big hug. John and their son Robert were behind her. "Merry Christmas, Bob," Lorrie said, but her eyes said more.

John said, "Let's all eat and go to the office. This is going to be the best Christmas ever."

We ate and then we all left, but after getting out the door, Brittany called to Mike to get the camera to get pictures of us all together and a picture of the four plus Misty. We headed for the office. It was hard for me to walk with Misty so close to me and Brittany holding on to me.

We entered the office and Brittany was already running to get a beer for everyone. "Aren't we starting a little early?" Tom asked.

"Hey, something good is happening, okay!" Brittany quipped.

"You better take your beer and not argue with her," Mark said. Besides, she is right!"

"Bob, we have started a new tradition here," Lorrie said. "We now do two toasts. The first is always to you, Bob and our second toast is to Christmas and we usually do this after the gift exchange, but today we make an exception. To Bob!"

"I didn't bring any gifts," said Bob. "All I have is pictures of places I've been." That is all I could say because I couldn't lie.

Tom stood up after the gift exchange and wanted to tell us something. "Brittany has not told us everything. Once again, her generosity has topped the list. Bob, you know how kind hearted and generous our Brittany is and she has really done it this time. Brittany is always doing things and never asks for help from anyone. She went and bought land just outside Salt Lake, a lot of land! She is building a home for all unwanted pets and abandoned animals. This is not a shelter but individual homes for the pets. They will not live in cages and will have enough room to run and play. There would be someone there 24 hours a day to make sure they were fed and get all the love they deserve. I asked her how much this was going to cost and Mark and Lorrie also offered to help, but she said she had it covered, but showed her appreciation to her friends for offering. She said she had received a cashiers check that covered all expenses and would pay all employees for years. We don't know who sent the check, but she is still trying to find out so she can thank them."

I smiled to myself as if I didn't know where that money came from.

Tom continued, "She put an article in the paper and invited anyone to come to her place to find a pet to call their own for a few hours or a whole day. She was aware of a lot of people who really wanted a pet but did not want the responsibility of caring for it, didn't have the time or people living in quarters that do not allow pets. The response was astonishing. Some would stop by after work for a couple hours and others spent the entire weekend. Brittany encouraged people with stressful jobs that a cute little pet for a few hours was a great relief for stress. The best part of this was it did not cost a dime to anyone. There was a donation box at the entrance and by doing that, Brittany discovered there were a lot of very generous people out there."

I got up and went over to Brittany and gave her a big hug. "Brittany," I said, remember when the President offered you a job in the White House. He has changed his mind. With your generosity, the government would go broke and even though good things were happening, there would be no money in it for the politicians and they won't that happen."

The day was coming to an end and all had left except for Mark, Brittany and Lorrie. I looked a them and told them how proud I was of them for all their work. "You have no idea of how many lives you have touched and I don't want any of you to ever give up hope." I remember our first article about the "mist" and the reaction of people around the world. Most were expecting some kind of miracle to happen and it didn't. They started to give up hope and lose patience. You three have never given up hope, but you need to do more. Keep writing and use the word RESPECT more in every issue and always have a little story about the "mist". The progress here is impressive and Lorrie, you have no idea of your potential. You have a special gift and don't realize it yet, but soon, you will. Keep your ears and eyes open and write about the things you see and hear. I'll be leaving tomorrow and will return next Christmas.."

We had a group hug and Lorrie walked me to my car. She whispered in my ear, "I think about you daily and I know you have a secret you can't talk about and that's fine. I understand."

I looked deep into her eyes and said good-bye and bent down to give a hug to Misty.

I left for Oregon the next morning and waited for the right time to assemble the vessel.

My trip back to the Island went smooth.

I went to the computer building the first day back. I told Joseph about my trip and what Brittany had done.

"Yes, I knew about that and was hoping it was a pleasant surprise to you." Joseph said. "What Brittany did was a good thing and this is what we will give our money to. If and when something like this happens, it will all be paid for. We won't run out of money and if we do we always know where we can get more."

The next month was devoted to the subject of converting ocean water into fresh water. Scientists from around the world had spent many years to come up with solutions but none had been found yet. This was one of the jobs for Sarah. She contacted the scientists and set up a place to meet. Half of the people she contacted to attend this meeting were young intelligent people working on the project. They were not known in the world of science and no college education but their committed interests in this project but bringing these people together would be the key to making this project work. They were brought together and starting comparing notes. They soon discovered a solution that worked. They spent weeks testing and using different ingredients and did find one mixture that was positive. The ingredients needed had to be gathered from many parts of the world. They all returned to their home and plans were set in motion to get their own governments involved. An agreement had been signed stating that no one country would take all the credit for the discovery and would be shared by the entire planet. These people stayed in contact with each other and agreed to get this water to the places needing it most. They all agreed that Africa would be where they were start.

The planning stage started with gathering people specialized in fields of agriculture, construction, marine bioligists and environments protection specialist. They would be able to get the water to anywhere it would be needed, building large reservoirs and planting crops where they never grew before.

Before they could start, setbacks set in. The human nature and greed. They only thought of the cost and how much they could make and never a thought of how humans and animals could prosper. These were government people and wealthy people with only dollar signs in their eyes. Joseph assured me that only good would come of this. The next elections would see to it that none of these individuals would be in office.

Joseph was setting in the computer building with other teachers and I asked to join them.

Joseph was saying, "This is all going to take time and it's all up to the people to make it happen."

"I hope it doesn't take too long because it's got people buzzing all over the world. The United States are always complaining and don't do much but complain." I said.

"Yes Bob," Joseph said. "That is why it will take a long time to see real change in the human race. Money is the problem and this is where we will start. The greedy only look at the bottom line and their decisions are made without looking at the changes to really be helpful to mankind. With the grouping of all the right people who are not lazy the project will be put in motion. The discovery of this new water is all they needed.

I spent a lot of time with the newcomers and always found time to spend with Star. We went to the ocean and talk to people about their work and new findings. Star and I would go to our favorite spot to play and relax. Our friend Lorrie did not join us today. Star ran up and down the beach barking at the water but our seal never came. I had a feeling we had lost our friend.

Another Christmas is here and I made my trip to Misty Mountain. It was a joyous occasion but the look in Lorrie's eyes bothered me. She kept telling me any secret I had would always be kept a secret with her. I gave her a hug and I sensed such a saddnes in her eyes. I really wanted to tell her everything, but couldn't. I took the latest issue of our magazine. When I arrived at the house in Oregon, I read Lorrie's stories and there was something missing but couldn't put my finger on it. I thought about it on my trip back to the Island.

I read the magazine over and over and took it to Joseph to read. He did not sense anything like I did. I explained that something was missing. It seems Lorrie is losing faith and confidence in her writtings and I blame myself. I explained the look in her eyes and she knows I'm keeping something from her. With all the love and respect we have for each other, she says she understands and I don't think she does. I would like to sspeak to everyone on the island tomorrow.

Thousands of people gathered for my speech and those not attending because of their duties would hear of my words within hours.

"I would like to thank you all for letting me stay here and make this my home." I started. "I want to talk to you about my friend, Lorrie. Joseph has told be she is an important key to the success of what you want to do with the world, but I feel like something is going wrong. I feel she is losing confidence in her work and I blame myself for that, by keeping things from her, but I know that has to be done. What I'm about to ask to everyone on the Island. I would like to bring Lorrie here to the Island for a few days. She needs to know about me. I trust her completely to keept our secret. She really needs to know about me to restore her confidence in her work. I do understand there are many things that must be kept secret from her but, I feel there are many things she can learn her that would help her. I can't make any decisions about what she can and can't do here on the Island while she is here, if you let me bring her here. I will wait for your input and even if one person says no, I will understand that this cannot happen. Thank you."

I went on with my normal activities and visited several people and their pets. Many gave me their opinions . This went on for three days. The teachers then came to see me.

The teachers were all smiling when Joseph said. "All the people have agreed to have Lorrie come here for a few days. We have drawn up a plan that you must follow at all times. There is a list of things that you can only say and do to Lorrie. The decision to come with you will be hers. When she arrives, there will be a list of where she can and cannot go and a list of what she cannot know about. Jan and you will spend all of your time with Lorrie. Something that we neglected to tell you about was one of our newcomers that spent a year with us tried to use what he learned here for his own benefit. When he awoke one morning, he was standing on a cliff looking out over a mist. He will continue to live his normal life without memory of his ordeals on the Island. Lorrie will be the only person to come here and when she returns, she will retain complete memory of her visit and we will have no way of erasing her memory. She must be reminded that everything she learns must always be kept a secret and will need your help in doing that.

"Thank you," I said. "Thank you all very much. You have no idea how much this means to me and Lorrie. I know the perfect time to arrange her visit. On Memorial Day every year, Lorrie goes alone to New Mexico to pay respects to her deceased grandfather. I think she would enjoy having a friend with her."

I was so excited when the time arrived. I stepped into the vessel and the trip seemed to take forever, but I remained patient and thought of what I was going to say to Lorrie. I arrived and took a nap at the house in Oregon and instead of driving to Misty Mountain, I headed for New Mexico.

I arrived early so went to have breakfast and made some phone calls and then drove out to the cemetery. I knew Lorrie would be there as she has never missed Memorial Day. I finally spotted her and got out of the car and walked towards her. About 10 feet away, I stopped and said, "Hi Lorrie, would you like some company?"

She was surprised to see me and said, "I would love some company." After a hug, we sat down. I put flowere on the grave and we talked for awhile. She told me her parents were buried here beside her grandfather. She wished she would have had more time with them.

Lorrie stood and asked if I wanted to go someplace to talk.

"Lorrie, please sit back down. There are many things I want to talk to you about and I can't think of a better place than right here. You are the best friend I've ever had and we have always been open and honest about everything. You have no idea how hard its been on me to keep secrets from you, but I had no choice. I want to make things right between us. When you came into my life, I saw something special in you and watched you grow and learn about my work. You have achieved special talent and I am very proud of you. Your words gave me inspiration, but in your last few stories, there seems to be something missing. I sense a loss of faith and confidence and belief. I hold myself responsible and am here to make things right. There are many things I can't tell you now and I think it would be better if I showed you and hopefully you will understand. I want you to come with me for a few days."

"Oh Bob, you have no clue of how long I've waited for this. Yes, I will go with you, I feel I must!"

We left the cemetery and asked Lorrie if she knew where we could get some pizza and find a park to eat and talk. She knew of a perfect place and off we went. When we got to the park, I told her I had called John and told him I was going to take you on a trip for a few days and he said it was alright and for you to call him. I also called the office and told Mark and Brittany that they would have to do without you for a few days. After Lorrie made her phone call to John, I began to tell her of my plans.

"Some things I'm about to tell you may freighten you. It frightened me a first but I knew I was taken to this place for a reason and waited patiently to find out why." I smiled at her and assured her it had nothing to do with space aliens and you are not going to be taken aboard a spaceship. It's a real place with real people. One secret that I must keep from you is where we go from here. I don't want to blindfold you so you must just trust me. I want you to take this harmless sleeping pill."

Lorrie said she wanted to go to her friends house to get her things and then said she will gladly take the pill.

"Are you claustrophobic?" I asked.

"No, why? She asked.

"This trip will be taken in a mininature submarine, but seats two very comfortably."

Lorrie laughed. "This is getting way to interesting. Let's get started!"

We left the park and went to her friends to pick up her things. I made the back seat comfortable so she could sleep. I gave her the pill and we left for Oregon.

We arrived early in the afternoon. I picked Lorrie up and carried her to one of the bedrooms and I went to the other bedroom to get some sleep. I woke up around midnight and went outside to make sure no one was around and assembled the vessel. I went in to wake Lorrie and she wanted to know where we were. I told her I could not tell her that. She got up and took a shower and I changed my clothes. She looked at me and I explained this is what we wear. It was dark so she couldn't see the landscape. We got into the vessel.

"This trip will normally take 20 hours, but I'm going to go slower. There is so much beauty down here and I want you to see things that no other human has seen. Enjoy the trip and ask me anything about the ocean." I told her.

"I'll just observe and please point out things to me and I'll just listen. Will we see any sharks or whales along the way?" She asked.

"Yes, and we will slow down so we don't bother them or any of the other beautiful creatures that live down here. There are a few things I am allowed to tell you before we get to the Island. We are going to an Island and it's where I've been since I left Misty Mountain. In case you are wondering about that night, I didn't jump off the cliff. When you and your husband drove away, John was waiting behind a tree and took me to his car. I did not remember anything about this and was told about it later. The Island is a very large island with about 300,000 residents. There are all races and all have love and respect for each other. They realize they need each other to make their community a beautiful place to live. You will see this when we get there. I was not the only one brought to the Island and I can not reveal the identities of the other four people. The five of us spent one year and learned many things. After the year the other four returned to their homes and I asked to stay. I knew this was best for me. It would have been so very hard on me to be around you daily and not be able to tell you the truth. Lorrie, all these people want is peace on earth and from what they have learned from me is that you will play a major role of protecting the earth and making it a peaceful planet. When I saw the last articles you wrote and sensed a lack of faith and confidence in your work, I asked the people on the Island if I could bring you to the Island for a few days. They all agreed. I need you to see for yourself that I'm doing well and releive doubts about me and to see for yourself why I must keep secrets from you. Please forgive me and I'm hoping you will understand.

"Bob, there is no need to ask for my forgiveness and I' m positive I will understand. The Island sounds like a beautiful place and I can't wait to meet the people. When I return home, will I have to keep this secret from my family and friends?"

"Yes, I'm sorry but it must be that way. You will understand why when you leave the Island. When you talk to your husband, John, choose your words carefully and I'm sure he will understand."

I pulled out a tray that had some food items and some pills. I asked Lorrie if she was hungry. I told her the snacks consist of her favorite foods. I urged her to try one and got us 2 glasses of water and dropped a pill in each glass. I loved the look on her face as she ate and could not believe it tasted like real food she was accustomed to . While she was eating, I sat the vessel down on the ocean floor. I pointed to a small box and mentioned that this was one of thousands throughout the oceans. We sat and watched as it collected plant life to be studied on the Island. They want every kind of plant life that grows in the oceans. We watched for awhile and then resumed our trip.

"We should be there in just a couple more hours," I said. "I want to tell you about the people. They are far more intelligent than anyone on this planet. After years of research, a combination of 1,147 ingredients, many from the ocean, the pills were made. The pills were tested and conclusions were that the pill must be taken every night by everyone. I have been taking this pill since I first arrived here. You can't believe how quickly you learn. After only 6 months, I could speak and understand every language known to man. You will not be given these pills. The Island is just ahead. Jan will meet us and you will go with her to meet Joseph. He is a teacher and taught me many things. I will not be going with you, but will join you later in the evening. They will tell you about their home and they want to do it without any influence from me. Don't be afraid and just let your curiosity take over. Listen carefully to everything Jan and Joseph say to you and I'm sure you will feel relieved and more relaxed."

We stepped out of the vessel and some of the scientists working nearby shouted, "welcome to our community, Lorrie." We waved back to them and Jan came up and said,

"Hi Lorrie, and welcome. You know, you don't look as scared as Bob did when he first came here."

We laughed and Lorrie said her thanks.

I was glad to see Lorrie start her visit with a laugh. "Jan will now take you to meet Joseph. Just don't turn into a Brittany and asking a lot of questions." We all laughed again and gave a hug and I told her I would see her later.

I watched as they drove off. I went to the beach to talk with Sophia. Sophia was excited about a new find from the north atlantic. The machine had been there many years. They needed the plants that only grow in that area for research, but they had died off because of oil spills. The plants are now starting to grow again and she stated these are very important in their work. I asked Sophia to inform me when the study would start with this plant, as I was eager to learn about this.

I went straight home. Jan told me that she would meet me there as soon as she left Lorrie with Joseph. Jan and I talked for awhile ans then rode to the shower together. When we returned to my house, I got a tray with food and pills and set in on my litlle table in the yard. About two hours before sunset, Joseph and Lorrie arrived.

"Joseph and I just came from the showers," Lorrie said. "Bob, you were right in keeping this place a secret from me. I do understand and your new home will always be a secret. I've never been happier for you than I am right now."

"While I'm preparing for a toast, there is someone else I want you to meet. Lorrie, this is Star."

Lorrie bent down to pet Star and said she really liked the name. "I started a new tradition back home and before we toast to all good things as to Bob. So, here's to Bob, his new home and new friends."

Joseph thanked Lorrie for visiting our Island. "I hope the things you learned today and what you will learn with Jan tomorrow with Jan will help you in your work. Good night and hope you will enjoy your visit."

"Tonight you will learn about the secret and its effect. You will soon see for yourself." I said to Lorrie.

The sun has just disappeared over the horizon the the music began to play. I told Lorrie to observe Star. He laid down and looked so peaceful.

"That is the most beautiful sound I"ve ever heard. I'm remembering all the pictures of dogs overlooking the mist over the years and is similar to what I am witnessing now. I'm just going to sit here and let you explain this to me."

'Yes, the effect is the same," I said. "It's not only the dogs, but all animals. It makes them all peaceful and relaxed. It wasn't until the end of my first year here that I learned all about the mist. The people here created the mist and can make it appear at any time at the nine locations on the earth. Each of the locations have small devices installed that produce the sound that you are hearing now. It is set a a low pitch and only affects the dogs. The people here have been searching for years for someone to make the connection of the mist to meaning something good and the dogs played and important part in connecting the two. It was the first couple issues of our magazine that brought us to their attention. They sent one of their travelers to Misty Mountain to observe and study us. After a couple years, they knew we were the ones they had been looking for. They planned for years on what they felt needed to be done. There are many people who are destroying the planet and many others who want to save it. Nuclear weapons are a major threat, but people here are not going to allow that. It's up to the people around the world to make our planet a safe and peaceful place to live. Many people believed in the mist at first, but their patience ran out. Five people continued to believe in the mist and these are the five that were brought here to the Island. This can be accomplished about the teachings of Respect. That is why you are here, Lorrie. No other person on earth knows as much about respect and you have a gift of putting it in words. You will get some help from the people that have been brought here and are now back home. Each one have goals and their main goal to to bring the right people together to work together to invent good things and make good discoveries. I know it will take hundreds of years to get to our goals and we won't be around to see the results. When bad things happen, look hard to write something good and when the bad things end, use the word respect in your stories.

"I'm not sure I c an do what you are asking of me," Lorrie said. "I would like to help in any way, but I don't think I am the right person for this. Sometimes I feel down and I might make a mistake and reveal something about the Island and that just can't happen."

"We are only asking you to do what you do best. Just remember the things I taught you when you came to work for us. Never be in a hurry, no deadlines and never let stress get to you. I've watched you grow into the beautiful person you are today. When you seem to get down, you have always looked into your heart and always found the answer you were seeking. You prayed and always found guidance from your grandfather and we both know he never let you down.. I've never mentioned that your job is very difficult. We watch TV and read newspapers and listened to so many stories at Tom's bar. I could never concentrate long enough to finish a story. We are only human and when we target only good things to write about with everything going on around us makes it most difficult. I found a lot of relief at the cliff with my dog. You, Mark and Brittany found another way to relieve your tensions by creating the dis-respect magazine. There are only 2 places on earth where I want to be, and that would be Misty Mountain and here on the Island."

Jan smiled at me and gave Lorrie a hug and told her she would show her the Island and said good night. I walked Lorrie to the main building where she was staying and urged her to sit outside and enjoy the evening music, gave her a hug and said good night.

Jan and Lorried toured the Island and Lorrie was amazed at the things she was learning. She loved the different landscapes in each section. The people did not crowd her, just stopped what they were doing long enough to smile and say welcome. She learned about the communication and the respect they had for one another. Jan took her to the school and the hospital and the playground that Bob had designed and told her all about the games they played. They toured the fields where the food was grown and how all the people would come to their sections during harvest time to help. The food processing building was next and Jan told her that the animal food was the first priority. Then the other foods for the people were made. Jan briefed her on the importance of the animals and how the animals depend on the people to feed them. The last stop of the day was at the ocean. Every drop of water on the Island comes from the ocean. Lorrie told Jan that she had heard of this process as it had been discovered in Africa. Jan explained that people all over the world were working on this. We felt they needed a little help. We sent people back from the Island and had them make contacts with all people involved in the research and bring them together and once that was done, the rest was easy. Jan said that many discoveries will be made in this process. By the process of bringing people from all over the world together and working together for something good will catch on.

The tour ended at the showers. Jan told her that there would be two things invented in the near future. By telling you this, we hope it will make you understand more clearly of how important that this must be kept secret at all times.

Jan and Lorrie arrived at Bob's house. Lorrie went in, walked over to the table to get a yellow pill and dropped it in a glass of water.

"So, how did your day go?" I asked Lorrie.

"Everything Jan has told me and the things I've seen really haven't sunk in yet." Lorrie said. I know there are things I can't see or learn anything about, but I think I understand. I know they are all good things or you would not be here. If you had told me about this place, I probably would not have believed you. I want to thank you so much for bringing me here to see things for myself. I do believe that what you are asking of me is very important and I hope I won't let you down." Lorrie then laughed and said, "If I wasn't married and believe I could do any of these things, you couldn't get me to leave."

We laughed together and Jan said, "About the two things I mentioned to you earlier and mention again that the secret must never be revealed, because they have not happened yet. One of these things is about the vehicle you have been riding in today and the other is about our waste system on the Island. We have found three people that have been working on these projects but, each one is missing something. We have to get these three individuals together and with their knowledge, they will benefit and compliment each other to find the solutions. The three people have something in common. They are all young and have no formal college or training but are the most intelligent in their fields. They are all employed by large corporations receiving hourly wages. The travelers from the Island will be sent back home and initiate bringing these three persons together. This is how it will be done. There is a science convention that many scientists are invited to attend. None of these three will receive an invitation from the committee, but will receive an invitation thanks to us. They will be seated together and we think they will become friends and compare their notes. They will discover the chemical that will be used to make all animal waste disappear into the ground. Only one has just recently made the connection of using the new water that comes from the ocean. Just think about this. When people take their pets for a walk, all they need is a spray bottle to make the waste disappear. We feel that it is very important that when you do your story about this and mention that three people from different countries become friends and have worked together to make something good. We have read the dis-respect magazine that you, Mark and Brittany publish. Some of the stories who you meet at the bar about bringing people together for a different reason. You listen always to their opinions and most are true, but are said in sarcastic humor.

People love reading this magazine because it gives them a big laugh. But, when people read Peace thru Respect, they take it more seriously and believe it to be good and true. We are confident that your words will make a tremendous difference. The second thing about the vehicles involves a lot of technology. Remember when you had a model airplane or car and could operate it with a remote control. In this computerized world, we were surprised no one has developed a car that is run on a computer chip. At an automobile convention, we will bring six people together in the same manner as we did a the science convention. Three of them will be there for the construction and design and don't have knowledge in the computer world. The other three that will be seated with them have been working on a computer chip that will run the vehicle. Together, they will make this new vehicle and it will meet every standard. It will be tested and retested and it will pass every test.

"Oh wow!" Lorrie exclaimed. "No more gasoline. I can't wait!"

"I wouldn't get to exited yet, Lorrie," Jan continued. We have done a little calculating just for the fun of it. In five years about 80% of the countries will have these new vehicles and no gasoline powered vehicles will be allowed. That will not be the case in the United States and will take 10 years or more. Just way to many people involved and rules and laws. If it will make you feel better, the first one made will be delivered to you at your office at Misty Mountain."

We sat and drank some beer and had a lot of laughs. Many people walked by to say hello to Lorrie . Before Jan left, she said tomorrow is her last day on the Island and a casual day is planned for the three of them.

I joined Jan and Lorrie the next morning and we drove down the main street to one end of the Island and turned around to go to the other end. We made several stops to the different sections and fed some of the animals. We ended at the ocean where I like to go with Star. Star ran up and down the beach, barking at the ocean. I told Lorrie that this is my favorite spot when I want to be alone. I always bring Star with me. One day a seal came up on the beach and Star barked at her. I named this female seal, Lorrie. The three of us became good friends. Every evening at sunset, Star would lay beside me and Lorrie began laying on the other side of me. It's been a few weeks since we have seen our seal friend and I feel we have lost a friend, but Star continues to bark at the ocean.

Lorrie jabbed me in the arm and pointed down the beach. "Is that your friend, Lorrie?"

I looked down the beach and was happy and relieved to see Star and

Lorrie playing again. "Yes, and look, now I know why she has been away. She has a baby with her. Come, lets sit and watch them. I had never approached her, always letting her come to me. Star ran to me and licked my face and Lorrie came and layed down in my lap. I looked down at the baby and said, "I will call you Brittany."

We watched the three play for awhile and then Lorrie took her baby and they disappeared into the ocean. We got up to leave and I suggested we return to my house because this is definitely a yellow pill moment.

It was still early so we took Lorrie to the entertainment building for a couple hours. Jan left us alone and said she would meet us in the morning to take us to the ocean.

"Well, Lorrie, I hope we have answered a lot of your questions and I apologize that we can't tell you more." I said. "I know there are things I have not learned about yet and I'm sure that I will be informed when the time is right."

"It's not what I've learned and seen here, but finally knowing about you and your secrets you've kept from me have made these past three days the best days of my life."

"There are some things I want to tell you about what we are asking of you but I'd rather wait and tell you when Mark and Brittany are present. Please be patient and you will understand.."

Lorrie went to sit by Star and asked me to sit with her as the music began to play. I saw the look in her eyes and it was good. I knew she had regained her confidence and there would never be any doubt about her work. This day came to an end to soon.

Jan met us the next morning to take us to our vessel. Lorrie thanked her and they had a good-bye hug. I thanked Jan and stated that this was exactly what Lorrie needed and we would be very proud of her work. We got into the vessel and began our journey.

We talked about the Island during the trip. About half way back, I told the sea was calm and we would surface in a few hours when it got dark. I wanted Lorrie to see the stars in the sky. It was a beautiful night and I told Lorrie when I return to the Island, I was going to learn about astrology and study the stars. When we submerged, I told her we were getting close and asked her to take the sleeping pill. We landed and I put Lorrie in a bed and then went and got some sleep.

I put sleeping Lorrie in the car and we bagan our trip to Misty Mountain. About an hour before we reached our destination, I pulled the car over to wake up Lorrie. "Good morning, we are almost home. You don't have any idea of how hard it is for me to ask of you what I need for you to do. I don't want you to lie to your friends, just find the right words to answer their questions. If they ask you where you have been, you tell them you have visited several places and met some of my friends and how you picked up hints on some stories you can write about. I have all the faith in the world for you and I know that our secret will always be safe. Now, you understand how hard it was on me when I came to visit."

Lorrie just held my hand and smiled. I told her that I would take some pressure off her after the four of us are alone and listening to some things I have to say.

We arrived around 10 AM and went to the office. After we got Brittany calmed down, we sat and talked about their work. I suggested we all go up to the cliff and mentioned I had some things I needed to say and the cliff would be the perfect place to do this.

I smiled and started by saying how very proud I was of each and the work they were doing. I read your articles and close my eyes and picture you all laughing and having a good time. I have a some suggestions to make that just may make you all more popular in the future. When I am finished, I'll explain why. First, I want to read more articles about people coming together to help those in need. I'll give you an example. A hurricane hit's the Gulf coast and people are coming to the aid of these victims. F.E.M.A., the Red Cross and the military come because that is their job. These are not the stories you should be looking for. It's about the victims coming together to help each other to re-build and others that have given up their time to come to physically help. All you see on TV and the newspapers is all about money. They put a price on the loss and a price of rebuilding. The government has a relief fund, but it is never enough. The victims need food, medical supplies and construction material. I don't know if the large corporations around the world help in any way, but see if you can find one that will take a loss and donate supplies that are needed. You hear about people donating food to the Red Cross and that is food purchased at the store. The large food manufacturing companies that may donate a check is not what to look for, but for the large companies that take a loss and send food at no charge and the same for medical supplies. Instead of a check, send the medical supplies. The same goes for the construction supplies. The kind of people we want to read about are the ones helping without putting a price on everything. It's about people coming together."

"Bob," Mark said, "I don't mean to interrupt, but I heard a cute story at the bar the other night. The subject was sports. Wouldn't it be great if every pro athlete would donate in some way when a disaster happens. Their contracts would contain a clause the they must go and physically help by cooking or doing construction. They would use their own transportation to get supplies needed and if the athlete did not go to help, 20% of his salary would be donated."

We all laughed. "Yes Mark." I said, That is exactly what to look for. As long as the story is about a human being and not a pro athlete. You know, that is one of the reason I quit watching sports. A pro does something not connected to sports and gets a lot of publicity. Those stories belong on TV, like in an episode on Law and Order, not on ESPN. I liked watching ESPN for sports scores and want to hear about sports and that just doesn't happen any more. Any wrong doing by a Pro will be broadcast often, day after day, week after week. People get tired of hearing about it.

"What another great story to our dis-respect magazine," Brittany says.

We took a little break and Mark went to get pizza. I asked him to stop by the office and bring back their address book.

After eating I showed them the address book. "This brings me to the second thing I wanted to discuss with you. Our friends from around the world are in this book and we stay in touch. I want you to work with them more often and listen to things they are doing in their countries to bring people together. The year of 2012 is not far away and we are all aware of the predictions that ancient civilizations and Nostradamus have made. We all have opinions on this. People like to expresss their opinions and there is always one to disagree. The arguments usually turn into a fight.. This almost happened when you first came to work for me. The only thing I did to prevent this was to get you to listen to each other and you learned how to deal with your decisions and work together. This gave you respect for each other and I could see that in every story written by you. Your knowledge of respect has reached millions around the world. A lot of people have learned from your stories and made their lives a lot richer. Some don't have patience and have lost faith. Since the beginning of time, fighting seemed to be the only answer they had for everything. Even though the country has progressed, people still find things to fight about. Nobody knows the future of our planet or about the predictions of our world ending in 2012. Some believe there will be a global disaster and no one would survive. If it's not global then it will be the people that will destroy the earth. If that's the case, some will survive. I only hope that anyone who believes that we have to fight for survival are the one's who don't survive, but the ones who have a strong will to survive are the one's we need to run our country, not just ours but every country. Peace thru Respect, let us only pray. Thank you for listening to me. Remember our ultimate goal and that is World Peace thru Respect and that will be realized in time and we will encourage this one story at a time. Little by little, it will happen some day."

We stayed at the cliff and everyone talked while I sat and listened. They all had one thing in common about their opinions and tht was that things will start to change long before December 21, 2012. When we got back to the office, I told them I would not be back for Christmas this year.

"Where are you going from here?" Brittany asked.

"I never told you before where I was going." I said. "You know how I like to spend time alone and my alone time helped me to regroup and find peace within. I've found places to spend my alone time. As for now, I think I'll take a long ocean voyage."

I glanced at Lorrie and she had a big smile on her face. We had a group hug and told them I'd see them in a couple years.

I was in the vessel headed to the Island and decided to surface to observe the stars. It was beautiful but I wasn't smiling, for I knew things were about to change.

Chapter IX

It's been a few months since my return to the Island. Not a day has passed without me thinking about the last thing I said to my friends that I would see them on Christmas next year and that date would be December 25, 2012. I do want to see my friends once again.

During my first week back, I'd asked Joseph if I could look at the stars through their telescope. I had never been to this room yet, so Joseph escorted me to the top floor of the main building and took me inside a room.

"Bob, I'd like you to meet Cindy". Joseph said. "Cindy is the expert in astronomy on the Island. There are several people who come here a couple nights a week, but Cindy is here every night which is why you have never met. Cindy is only 16 years old and knows everything about the stars."

"Hi Bob", Cindy said. "It's about time you came to see me."

I laughed. "It's nice to meet you. I can't believe that I have spent my entire life ignoring something as beautiful and mysterious as the stars in the sky."

"I'm going to leave you two alone." Joseph said. "Cindy can explain everything you want to know, especially about the galactic alignment of the planets and the sun and what this means in relation to the predictions of December 12, 2012. Another secret we have kept from you is about 2012. I guess now is a good time to reveal this to you. We do know that the alignment of the sun and the planets will have an affect on the planet but don't know the extent of this affect yet. If the worst happens, not all the life on the planet will be lost. Our Island will not be affected at all. We will survive on the Island."

Joesph left and Cindy told me she would show me around. "As you can see, there is no roof in this room. There are ten telescopes and they are permanently placed and a computer connected to each one. If you want to look at something else, we use these." She handed me a smaller one to look through. "These smaller telescopes are 10 times stronger than any other on the planet. Here is something that might interest you." She handed me a picture. "If you were to travel in an exact orbit around the sun, you will see that there is only one planet that is the same distance from the sun other than our planet. We do know the atmosphere is the same as ours and there is life there but we do not know what kind of life form. All the other planets are aligned completely different from ours, but this one planet is being constantly watched and studied. We know how unstable our planet is and we are hoping this new planet is more stable. There's another thing I want to show you and your timing couldn't be more perfect. This is another picture I want to show you. It is all black, but tomorrow night at around 11, you will see a little sparkle and it will turn into a bright shining star within a few minutes and will be visible to the naked eye for 3 hours before it turns to darkness again. This star can only be seen by the naked eye on this day every year. We don't have any answers for this yet. Just come back tomorrow night and see for yourself."

"Thank you Cindy. I will be back tomorrow night. Since this is all new to me, I'll probably have a million questions for you. I'm very excited and I feel like I'm reborn into a whole new world."

The next night I was at the observatory to observe this star. I watched for three hours and watched it disappear. I became a real regular and would spend a few hours every night and one night every week, I'd spend the entire night. This was so fascinating.

It was now 2011 and people are now becoming aware of what the future might bring. The earthquakes, tsunamis, volcanic eruptions, hurricanes, tornados or even a slight change in the temperature has more people saying, what could be happening. There are a few people who built underground shelters a few years ago and now there are more people building these shelters. Later in the year people with these shelters started buying large quantities of food to stock their shelters. Prices were going up rapidly. People got together to protest the rising prices of food but that didn't stop the rising prices. People started looting grocery stores everywhere all over the country. The police called in the National Guard and could not stop this. The military joined in and it became chaos everywhere. Trucks delivering food were robbed, even with military escorts. Starving people were desparate and were obtaining food in any way they could. It was like a war had broke out. The worst thing about all this. Mark with the help of his father had messages sent to every state capitol and the White House. They had millions of signatures on petitions asking them not to raise food prices. This was done before the prices were increased, but it did no good. This war went on for months and then the President addressed the nation. Everyone was listening when he announced the food prices would go back to normal and in many cases less cost than before and this is effective today. He said many trucks were loaded and asked for people to be patient. This food would be free and distributed to those desparately in need first.

It was way to late, for there were many supermarkets completely destroyed and the people still outraged at what their country did to them. What has happened will not be forgotten because their were more casualities than any war since the beginning of man. Most of these people killed were innocent and worked for minimum wages and had no choice. They would rather fight for food than starve to death. And why did this happen? Greed in the food industry and why the President did not stop this earlier, no one knows.

Another letter was sent to the state capitols and the President. It was more of a statement that blamed every person in grocery rising prices to be considered a mass murderer, just because of their greed. Then the greedy ones mysteriously lost every penny they had.

The year of 2012 has arrived and no one has learned a lesson about the tragedy they have just went through. More and more fighting was breaking out all over the world. Every country was put on red alert. There was little patience and no respect. People would panic at every earthquake, hurricane, tornado. The real panic started in the oceans. A U.S. submarine detected a Russian sub had just launched their missiles and every sub around the world launched missiles. Even on the ground, every button was pushed to launch every missile they had. What happened later or what didn't happen put the entire world in a state of shock. Every missle that was launched by the submarines was disarmed and sank harmlessly to the bottom of the sea and every ground missle they tried to launch was disarmed and not one missle ever left the ground.

It is now December 2012 and another nightmare is about to occur. Over the past few years, the terrorists had secretly hidden over 100 nuclear weapons. They were going to commit mass suicide and destroy the earth. All the terrorists gathered around the bombs and pushed the buttons at the same time. Every bomb was set to go off in 5 minutes. When the countdown hit zero, nothing happened. Within those 5 minutes, authorities all over the world were notified of the location of the bombs and the terrorists were all arrested. This sent a shock throughout the terrorist world.

The date is December 21, 2012 and the galactic allignment did take place and did cause some natural disasters, but the earth and the people did survive. Everyone was aware that things could get worse at any time. I knew it was safe and I prepared for my trip to Misty Mountain. About a hundred yards from the Oregon coast, I detected that the Oregon house had been destroyed by an earthquake, so I headed up to our Canadian home. I took my nap and then turned on the TV to catch the details of the Presidents speech from the day before. It was a long speech and I paid attention to the most important part. Every leader from every country agreed that all nuclear devices would be disassembled and never again would anyone develop anything that could be used as a mass destruction device. It was agreed on and signed by all.

My reunion was not as happy this time. A lot of sadness and they didn't have much to write about. I found time to be alone with Lorrie and she told me she knew who was responsible for saving the planet and no one will ever know. She wished we could have done more, but she knew we couldn't.

"Lorrie, it will take time for everyone to recoveer and I know now there is nothing good to write about, but there are many good things in the future, some good and some not so good. The not so good things will become good things long after we are gone. The world needs you now and please talk with your foreign friend as much as you can.

Christmas night turned out to be a very special night. For one hour, around the world, a candle burned in every house on the planet. Not a word was spoken during this hour. If there ever was a meaning to Peace on Earth, this was the time.

We had a hug but no toast and many tears fell that night.

I left the next morning. I stopped in several small towns on my way back to Canada. I listened to the people discussing the past year and all that happened. They were discussing what they could do to prevent bad things from happening again. A couple towns, there was only one store to buy groceries and in both towns the owners had left town. I drove by the location of our Oregon house. The house had been completely destroyed by the earthquake. I also noticed the water level was about 2 foot over what it used to be. I wondered if it was over or just the beginning.

During my trip back to the Island, I looked for changes on the ocean floor. I did notice a few and wondered if they would have any effect on the earth. I made myself a mental note to pay more attention to weather patterns and climate changes. I was also going to look at the stars and see if there was any difference in the alignments. Our planet has survived, but for how long? Something could happen tomorrow, ten years or in a hundred years. Nobody knows but we do know there be a change and it could destroy the earth.

I spent my first days back with the teachers and they knew something would happen in 2012. They told me people have survived and hope they can learn from it and will have to adjust to what lies ahead.

I went on with my usual routine. I'm waiting patiently to read the next issue of Peace thru Respect magazine. I was spending a little more time in the computer building and was kept up to date on the happenings around the world, mainly in the United States. Everyone around the world knew what caused all the chaos and were beginning to find ways in their political policies that would prevent these things from ever happening again. The United States was running far behind other countries in their progress, but in early spring of 2013 the whole political system was about to change. First, the President fired several people and resigned. The Vice President resigned shortly after. There was one voice in congress listened to and respected and that was a voice of a woman. The election was coming up later this year and without a doubt, this woman would be elected.

During the next few months many people were back on their jobs. The supermarkets and grocery stores were being rebuilt and food was available to everyone again. With the discovery of the new water system, scientists were making many new discoveries with new chemicals that will benefit everyone. There was a big clean-up that had to made on the west coast before they could start the installation of the pipe lines that will reach all the mountain regions that are vulnerable to forest fires. If a forest fire would start, it would quickly be controlled by the new sprinkler systems. New businesses were popping up and the biggest one was the automobile manufactures.

Many people began to plant small gardens and experienced gardeners helped the first time gardeners. The new chemicals would keepe the harmful insects away as well as other animals that would normally feed on their gardens. Large areas of land near the small towns were turned into farmlands. The farmers had lost faith in the government, but started farming again and were determined to prevent a tragedy that they had just recovered from. They all told themselves that this would never happen again.

It was during this year that the doctors around the world finally came to the conclusion that after a woman gave birth, she could no longer give birth again. At first when women visited the doctor and wanted to get pregnant and tests were given and the doctors said they were all healthy and they did not look further because other women were getting pregnant. But then the doctors started asking the women if they already had a child and in every case they did and that was the reason they could not conceive again. This was the case around the world. This made the news and sex education classes were inducted in every school. The parents of the daughters would stress the importance of starting relationships. The men thought they could take advantage of this situation. If the girl already had a baby, they would not have to worry about getting her pregnant. More cases of rape were happening. New laws were immediately enforced. A man convicted of rape would be sentenced to life with no chance of parole.

The day finally came later this year when the new edition of Peace thru Respect magazine came out. After I read all the stories, I then knew what Joseph meant by Lorrie being the key person they were depending on. The way she had with words was truly remarkable. The stories were short and simple about people coming together to help each other and never a price on anything. These amazing stories caught the eye of the President and she called the office and thanked them.

Later on this year, five people came together to form a business that will affect how all businesses will be run in the future. The three people that discovered the chemical that made animal waste disappear went to get a patent on their product. After two of them returned to their countries, the other one and two of his friends quit their jobs at the chemical plant. They found out that the company was going to take all the credit for their discovery. Two women who worked in the office were experienced in the world of business and they handed in their resignations also. The five of them got together and drafted up a plan to start their own company. They needed a loan and showed their plan to the banker. They were approved immediately. The three people who actually discovered the spray had sent seeds from their plants that was only found in their country. With the help of the new water, all three of them could grow their own plants in their own yards. This would save them a lot of money. They rented a large building for their lab and factory. People who came in to apply for a job was handed a paper before they were given an application. The paper listed qualifications that they would have to meet.

1. You must be able to speak and understand the English language.
2. You must have a high school education.
3. You must be an American citizen for at least 10 years.
4. Since we work with chemicals and assembly lines, communication with your fellow empoyees is the most important part of your job. Only one language is to used. This shows respect to your co-workers.

There were many discrimination acts filed and not one of them stood up in a court of law. Those that were hired came in for their orientation. They were all amazed at what they heard. Some pinching was going on to make sure they were not dreaming. They were informed they would only work 4 days a week and 8 hours a day. Every one will be on a 60 probation. Being late or missing work will not be tolerated. We understand about emergencies but if they occur often, they become excuses to miss work. We have an incentive that will make you want to come to work and be on time. After your 60 day probation, you will become a full partner and that will be explained after the 60 days. Missing work and tardiness shows disrespect and that will not be tolerated at any time. After the 60 days, you can come in on your day off, Friday and learn about our operation. You will be shown the books and see what we spend and how much we make. You will learn about shipping and receiving and may drive our trucks to make deliveries to our stores. You can learn everything about the company. You may exchange jobs with others. We are all equal, but one job everyone is responsible for is the janitorial work. You are responsible for cleaning up after yourself and will never leave a mess for someone else to clean.

These five people want to make a statement to the entire business world. The goal is to have the lowest turn-over ratio ever recorded in history. Whenever the word money is mentioned, the word greed will never apply, for we know what greed can do.

The world is still in shock over the events happening in 2011 and 2012 and the world leaders began making changes. The first one involved the United Nations. Every country is now a member of the U.N. A treaty was signed and mostly stated that each country would show respect towards one another and let each country make decisions on how to run their country. All military personnel would return to their own country. There would be no interference between countries and helping one country with money or weapons will not happen. If any country is at war with a neighboring country, crossing borders would be halted by a military force consisting of military personnel from every country ran by the United Nations. They would arrest the people responsible and then leave it up to the people to make changes in their governments.

In less than two monlths, every military person serving in the armed forces of the United States have been returned home. At first, they thought there would not be enough facilities for jobs for them. That didn't last long. Every state will have a new base for each branch of the military as well as their own basic training camps. The military would build 30 new bases for the military personnel who would be employed by the U.N. and it would be these people who will be sent to where trouble erupts.

Drugs were still a problem, but hard to find and very expensive. The drug situation still caused problems in schools and the city. Many of the soldiers that returned home and only about 5% re-enlisted. Others returned to their homes to help their families and the cities to fight crime. With many people leaving the military and few enlisting, the military was not as strong as the President wanted it to be. She resorted to the old days of the draft. If you were drafted, you would do your basic training in your home state. You would be on active duty with the National lGuard. A lot had heard stories about the draft and many moved to Canada to avoid the draft. But this time many would go to Mexico instead of Canada. Even though the Mexican government had cracked down on drugs, they were still easier and cheaper to get them. The President received a lot of criticism for bringing back the draft but it was something she and her staff could live with.

During the next year, I noticed there were no newcomers being brought to the Island. I found Jan and we sat down for a long talk. She told me that everything they had started out to do was completed. When the people completed their assignments, their memory was erased about everything they had learned on the Island and they would continue to live a normal life. It's all up to the people now.

I changed my routine and stopped going to the computer building because it reminded me of all the tragedy that people had went through. I thought about my home and all I could think about was my friends at Misty Mountain. I spent most nights with Cindy and the stars and my days were mostly spent at the ocean with Sophia. I never missed an evening waiting for the sunset and enjoying watching my three friends play. Each day I would wait for the new issue of our magazine. I'd read two more issues and they brought tears of happiness to my face. I really understand what Joseph meant by Lorrie being the key. Jan came to the ocean and said she had news for me. She handed me a copy. It was from the office in Misty Mountain. They had received a telephone call from the President and told Lorrie she was to be awarded the Nobel Peace Prize. I began making plans to go to the White House to be with her.

John returned to the Island, this time to stay, for his job was complete. We started to visit the entertainment center because this is where John always went after his trips. It was good to have him home as I valued our discussions. I thought John was the only one I could sit with and talk about things back home, but later I learned that I could talk to anyone on the Island. John's opinions always meant more to me.

It was about a week before my trip to Washington D.C. and for the first time I was allowed to use one of their computers to send a message to Lorrie. I told her how proud I was of her and that I would meet her in Washington D.C. John informed me that this trip would be my first to the house in Maine and would take me a little longer to get there.

I was standing at the airport talking to the people that would escort my friends to their hotels. Their plane was landing and I went out to meet them. Lorrie ran to me first and I got a big hug, followed by Mark and Brittany. I saw John and Robert and my eight friends from around the world. We got to the hotel and settled in and then gathered in one room for a visit. Someone asked Lorrie about her speech.

"When I first received the news, I was just so excited." Lorrie said. "I first wrote a little something and then stopped. I knew that all 12 of us should be together for this. When they called me and asked how many people would be joining me and I told them 14. I really couldn't find the words and as of now I still don't know what to say but I knew it will be easier with all of you here with me.."

"Ever since I've known you and since you are better with words than anyone else, you really don't know what to say." Brittany said.

That statement from Brittany had everyone in the room laughing. We called it a night and went to our rooms for a good nights rest.

Morning came and we were taken to the White House. After going through all the security, we were taken to our seats. Lorrie joined the people on the stage. The President was announced and joined Lorrie on the podium. She made a short speech and introduced the committee that was to award this award to Lorrie. She then introduced Lorrie. When the applause died down, Lorrie asked if her 11 friends could join her on the stage. Lorrie introduced us one at a time and we stood with her.

Lorrie began her speech. "I know that there are some people up here that you don't recognize, but you should. None of our stories would have ever been published without all of us working together. First, I couldn't have written anything without the help of my best friends, Mark and Brittany. The biggest part of our success comes from my eight friends that do the same kind of work in their own countries that we do. Together we share all of our stories and that is why I can not accept this award."

There were a lot of confused people in the room. While Lorrie was talking, Brittany was looking at the people in the room and noticed some people whispering to each other.

Lorrie continued, "The most important person responsible for this is my best friend, Bob. This magazine was Bob's dream. He hired us and taught us all about Respect. When the first story about the mist appeared, it was Bob who traveled to all the different countries and met these special people. He is the one that brought us together to make our magazine a success. I refuse to accept this award because it should be awarded to all of us."

The President brought order to the room and asked the 12 of us to join her in the oval office. John stood up and introduced himself and stated he was very proud of his wife and was asked to join the rest with their son Robert in the oval office.

Lorrie apologized for all the comotion she had caused.

Brittany asked if she could speak and was allowed. "Madame President, I sensed a little commotion when we were brought up to the stage. Look at us. We are all so different. I mean, we are all wearing a sweatshirt bearing the Peace thru Respect logo, blue jeans and tennis shoes. I'm different and proud of it. You know, if I was to go back out there and put a sack over everyone's head they would all look identical."

Once again, the way Brittany expresses herself made everyone laugh.

The President stood up. "If I had known ahead of time, I would have had the committee and myself dress like you. Please excuse me for a few minutes. I would like to talk to the people."

Mark stood up and handed the President a sweatshirt.

"Thank you, Mark, but while I'm President I couldn't wear this shirt because I would not receive respect from everyone. I will hang it proudly in this office and look at it daily.

Our friend from China stood and said, "Madame President, if you ever come to my country, feel free to wear the sweatshirt proudly."

"Thank you. Now, please excuse me. I have some people to talk to and when I return, I promise that there will be an award for each of you with your name on it and everyone who works with you. It will be delivered to your offices by the leader of your country personally."

After the President left the office, I asked the others to stay for a few days. "I have visited your countries and I would like to show you our beautiful country.

The President returned and said everything she promised would be fulfilled. She thanked us. I asked her if she could do us a favor. I said since the new vehicles that are run by a computer card are out now and I noticed you had a 30 passenger bus built especially for you. I would like to know if I could borrow it to drive it to Los Angeles to show our foreign friends our beautiful country. She agreed to let us do that.

When we got back to the hotel, we had a toast. I discussed the route we would take to California. Our first stop will be Niagra Falls, and then through some of the cities in the great lake area. We will go through the heartland and I asked if anyone enjoyed a good steak. They all loved steak so I told them they would be treated at Omaha, Nebraska for one of the best steaks in the world. We will then see Mt. Rushmore and go on to Yellowstone National Park. We will also visit Lake Tahoe, Las Vegas, the Grand Canyon and before we end our trip at the airport, we will spend a day at Disneyland.

This trip was enjoyed by everyone and commented it was very fascinating. We had a final toast at the airport and we said good by. I flew back to Maine and headed back to the Island.

I took Star to the ocean my first day back and after the sunset, went to the entertainment building where I met John and we discused my trip.

A few years have passed and Star was put to sleep. The next day, I had a new dog that I named Mark. I took him to the ocean to acquaint him with Lorrie and Brittany. It was fun to watch them play together and reminded me of my friends at home.

Another few years flew by and I returned to Misty Mountain, not knowing this would be the last time I would be with my friends.

I wasn't feeling well upon my return to the Island and went to see the doctor. The doctor said my body was dying and nothing could be done. I was told I had about 4 months to live. John took me to the library and into a secret room and gave me books to read. In just one month, I read all the books. All the mysteries of our planet was in these books. I learned about ancient civilizations and strange landmarks around the world. I learned the secrets of the pyramids. The most interesting was stone henge. Everyone knows about it but no one has a clue about it's existence. I learned that it is not complete and it will not be completed until all human beings are ready to accept the secret it holds. It became clearer now about what the people on the Island have set out to do and why they say it's up to the people now. If the people on earth ever meet the standards of peace on earth, it will then be the people from the Island that will complete stone henge.

I wrote a letter to John with a list of things I would like for him to do. He looked it over and said he would meet every request. I also wrote 3 letters, one for Lorrie, and one for Mark and one for Brittany. I gave these letters to John to deliver to them.

The day had come for John to take me back to the United States and let me die there. When John reached the mainland, I was very weak and John took me to the nearest hospital. One of the nurses recognized me. They did everything they could for me. Bob died in the middle of the night.

John followed the instructions from Bob and after a couple days headed for Misty Mountain. The word of Bob;s death had reached Misty Mountain and it was a very sad time. John headed for the office and they all remembered John and had a group hug. John told them he was there with Bob when he passed and he wanted me to come here and ask them to join him on the cliff. They drove to the cliff. John told them that he was here to grant Bob his final wishes. He handed a letter to Mark, another to Brittany and one to Lorrie. Mark was the first one to read his letter.

Dear Mark,

I have never met anyone at such a young age who learned so quickly and so much about respect. You have always been a special friend and I know I could not have accomplished the job without you. Even at your young age, you had a dream about running your own press and you made it happen. Many great stories read around the world and every one of the words were run on your press. I'm so very proud of you and I love you.

Brittany read hers next.

Dear Brittany,

It's so hard to describe how I really feel about you. I guess I can sum it up in two words. The first word is generous, the most generous gal on earth. Heart is the other word. You have the biggest heart of anyone I know. If there is such a thing called the fountain of youth, I have renamed it Brittany's Pond. People have said that laughter adds years to life. If that is true, then every person who has ever come into contact with you has added at least 10 years to their lives. I'm so very proud of you and I love you.

Lorrie opened her letter.

Dear Lorrie,

I've always had a special place in my heart for you. I never thought you knew enough about how I felt about our friendship, our trust and the respect I have for you. These things can never be duplicated by any two people on the planet. I have enclosed a special gift for you. It's a picture of the stars in the sky. If you look at this picture, you will see that I have circled a little spot on it. I want you to study this on every clear night. Only one night a year, you will see a little sparkle and then a bright shining star will appear. It will only be visible for 3 hours on this one night. You will notice the date and that is the same date your grandfather passed away. I'm so proud of you and I love you.

The mist suddenly appeared over the valley and John took 4 beers and let Brittany pass them to everyone. He then took out the cannister that held Bob's ashes. Before they toasted they heard the music softly playing. The sound got louder and louder and everyone in Misty Mountain stood in the streets listening to it. As John held up the cannister, the three special people touched their cans to the cannister. John opened the cannister and let Bob's ashes float out over the mist.